Cursed Kingdom

Titles by J. L. Jackola

Unbound Prophecy Series
Ascension
Descent
Surfacing
Submerged
Riven
Adrift

Unbound Kingdom Trilogy
Severed Kingdom
Cursed Kingdom

Cursed Kingdom

Unbound Kingdom Book Two

J.L. Jackola

Tivshe Publishing

Copyright © 2022 J. L. Jackola

Library of Congress Control Number 2022911058

ISBN 978-1-954175-41-9

Distributed by Tivshe Publishing

Printed in the United States of America

Cover design by Dark Queen Designs

Map design by Worldwyrm

Visit www.tivshepublishing.com

To the ones lost to me. The void is never completely filled.

TENEBRON
GAERNEM
western coast

CIRILLIA

One

The room was silent save for the pounding of Xali's heart. The beauty of the peaceful gardens stood in contrast to the tumultuous emotions that stormed within her. Carnick stood to her left, the remains of their family behind them, all awaiting their sentences.

The Dark king stood before them, the Light queen at his side. Their son Ren had taken his place to the left of them with the auburn-haired woman Xali had surmised was his wife, while the king's brother stood to the right with his mate, Chastity. Men in capes, the colors of both black and white, flanked Xali and her family in two long columns.

Xali peeked back at her father, his eyes defiant, face stoic. The others stood proud, huddled beside each other. Carnick took her hand, and she met his stormy eyes. Would this be the last time she'd look into them, the last she'd feel the strength of his hand around hers? It seemed like just yesterday she was innocently anticipating her joining with him, unaware that her uncensored curiosity would lead them here. Now, they stood, awaiting their sentencing, the impending death that curiosity had caused.

The queen moved from her husband's side, the king's eyes following her. Her motion was soundless and magical giving the illusion that she was floating. Xali swallowed loudly as the queen stopped in front of her, her brilliant emerald eyes evaluating Xali. She wanted to scream for forgiveness, to plead that they'd righted their wrongs by waking her and the other immortals, that her family shouldn't be punished, but she stayed silent.

"Xaliandri," the queen's enchanting voice said, the sound drifting to Xali's soul and calming her nerves.

She brought her hand to Xali's hair and softly ran her fingers along a lock that had fallen to cover part of her eye. Xali had been too full of trepidation to move it, afraid the motion would reveal her shaking hands. The queen pulled the lock out, letting it gently fall back to place then took her fingers and pushed it from Xali's eyes, her fingers then tracing the corner of her eye, lingering. There was a strange intimacy to it, as though her mother were standing before her, appraising her.

"You carry the traits of the Mother Fate, I see her in you, yet your stormy eyes belie your tie to her Dark lover."

Xali wasn't certain what to say, the words leaving confusion in her mind.

"Children of the Fates just as the Dark and Light, just as the Elvin."

Her eyes morphed to a rich sage, and Xali had to keep herself from stepping back in surprise. It was fascinating to watch yet terrifying at the same time. Where the emerald held kindness and curiosity, a calm that left her feeling she could lose herself in their beauty, their sage held more, an ancient knowledge, a sense of power that held judgment, one that could be kind but also cruel if that judgment warranted. The queen was more than the delicate woman she appeared to be, much more, and Xali knew in that moment that she was one to never underestimate, for there was a dangerous side to her beauty and calm, one that held a wrath only her enemies had known.

"You are children of our world, yet ones of myth. The result of a love that was cursed to never be." The queen turned her head and glanced toward the king. "One which was healed through pain and suffering, bound by prophecy to correct the wrongs, the mistakes…" She looked back at Xali, her eyes a blend of emerald and sage. "You are a conundrum, Xaliandri. Everything we thought we knew, you defy, yet here you are, a beautiful blend of two races, gifted from the Mother Fate with nature magic, and from her Dark lover his Dark magic. The combination creating a new magic that warps the two into something destructive if not understood, yet in you who senses both sides of it, something beautiful."

Xali, whose head was spinning, her tongue sore from restraining her myriad of questions, finally spoke, unable to refrain any longer.

"I don't understand, what do the Fates have to do with my family?"

Carnick squeezed her hand, silently trying to keep her quiet. The queen studied her for a moment, her eyes shimmering back to the light green before she smiled.

"Everything, my child." She touched Xali's hair again. "You are children who lost your way, punished for the actions of your creators, punished by a vindictive Fate, cast aside from those the other Fates felt were their true children, ripped from the Mother Fate's arms. They cast your people out for what they saw as her sins, what they were manipulated into believing by a brother Fate who held nothing but jealousy and anger at the Mother Fate for loving another. Over time, your people chose to forget their origins, forget that it was she who had pleaded for your lives to be spared, that it was by her hand you are still here. Over time, the hatred for the Fates who cast you out left them forgotten, replaced with false idols, your history erased until finally Drakine vowed we should be punished for what we were given, and he was not: the blessing of the Fates."

She turned from Xali and walked away.

"How is any of that our fault? Why do the sins of a man who we only remember through history become our sins to bear?" Carnick's mother asked.

Xali cringed, knowing the question was not one that should have been asked in this company but one all of them had on their minds. She held her breath as the queen stopped her path back to her husband's side. When she turned back, the hues of her eyes were as deep as the forests, close to the black the king's had turned.

"Because you perpetuated the lies, the mistreatment of our people, all so you could continue to falsely rule a land that was never yours," the king answered for his queen. A black haze now surrounded him, changing the mood in the room abruptly.

Xali decided to step in. "It's true, Drakine wronged you and your people. Our family following his lead, never questioning as we should have, never doing what was right."

"Xali," her father whispered, trying to silence her.

"Ten thousand years he ripped from us," the king said while the haze spread. "In that time, he nearly decimated the population of three races, all for what? Power? Revenge?"

"Revenge for crimes which he felt you deserved punishment. Just as you now lay that same judgment on us!" Xali cried.

He stepped toward her, his eyes an endless void of terror. The darkness suffocated Xali, and she tried to fight back, but it enveloped her soul, clawing its way in so that she couldn't breathe, couldn't move. In that moment, she knew why his people had feared him, a part of her admiring it, rising to meet the pain, the fear that was pummeling her very desire to live.

"Leave her alone!" she heard Carnick, but his last word was cut off as the king's power punished him as well.

She heard her father begin to object, but then her aunt's voice quieted him. "This is Xali's fight," she said, her words strengthening Xali.

Xali forced her eyes to continue staring at the king, understanding that he expected her to avert her eyes, expected her obedience, just as they all had, her entire life. She was tired of staying obedient, of never being able to speak up, of always being told she was meaningless, cursed, simply a second born.

Time seemed to stand still as he continued to stare her down, the pain intense. Then she realized, this was not only a punishment; it was a test. He was testing her, but to what end?

"I will no longer be subservient," she said through gritted teeth. "The crimes of my ancestors are not my crimes to bear. Kill me if you must, but I will not lay claim to deeds which I do not own. I have made my choice, I made it the moment I began to question."

Talking was an effort, and a bead of sweat dripped down her brow.

"And what choice was that?" he asked, his voice deep with power.

The little girl in her wanted to turn and run, to have nothing to do with this terrifying man. The warrior in her refused to turn, standing against the rising tide that threatened to drown her, to mentally collapse her until there was no sanity left.

"To find the answers, to find you, to free you and right the mistakes of our past, no matter the cost."

The queen moved to her husband's side, and Xali watched the change in him as she laid her hand on his arm. He softened instantly like a calming blanket had been lain upon him. The pain fled, and Xali inhaled deeply, her lungs filling again. Then she felt the soft tingle of healing magic, her body relaxing, her own mind calming at the queen's touch.

The king approached Xali, his now dark brown eyes holding something that looked like pride.

"You are brave, child. The Darkness in you calls to be used. You will need to learn to heed it as you use your powers." He looked at

Carnick. "And you hear its call too loudly. It is your nature side that needs to find its place."

With that, he turned and walked back to stand with the others. The queen took Xali's hand then Carnick's. "You found us, and for that, we will eternally be grateful."

The queen looked down at their hands, her eyes getting a far-off look. "What your family has done goes against the laws of nature. Forcing the Fates hand by marrying blood to blood. The Fates punished Drakine for his indiscretions by giving him multiple heirs, stripping his full power down in that next generation, lessening it by design. By marrying kin to kin, your family has forced their hand, the power still diminished, split between eight in each generation, but stopping the diminishment. Kin to kin is an affront to nature, a slight in the eyes of the Fates, and his children knew that when they began the practice. It ends with you."

There was an uproar from her family until the king's voice boomed, "Silence!" and they all fell to their knees. Xali could feel their pain as his power engulfed the room.

"Stop him, please," she begged the queen. The queen's eyes shifted to the distance, and then Xali felt the Darkness lift. The queen had said no words, but somehow he'd heard her. Had they spoken in their heads? She still couldn't believe it was possible, but Xali was finding there were many impossible things tied to the immortals.

The queen's eyes evaluated Xali's family before they turned back to her.

"Thank you," she whispered.

The queen didn't respond. Instead, she reached out and touched Xali's hair again. "So like her. She loved your people, her children, and they turned their back on her." Her eyes held that faraway look again, growing a shade deeper. "It is time to right the indiscretions, to bring you back into the fold." She focused back on Xali, dropping her hand. "It is time for sentencing."

Xali's heart fell. With the queen's talk, there had been hope, a sliver of chance they would be forgiven. But with her final words, that hope crumbled. There would be no forgiveness, no chance to prove they were different.

As the queen walked back toward the king, Xali looked at Carnick, meeting his eyes. They were filled with worry, the storm clouds encompassing his pupils. She pulled her eyes away as Ren walked toward them, Carnick's hand slipping to hers.

"As I will soon take the throne, and your Fate impacts my reign, the decision as to your punishment has been left in my hands. My father and mother have offered their advice as have their Councils and my uncle, but the ultimate decision is mine."

Xali swallowed, awkwardly loud, her breath stuck in her chest. This was it; this was the moment. Their lives were now in the hands of this one man. It didn't seem possible or even fair that one man should hold their fates, either granting or taking their lives in a single swift move. Yet had not the same been done by the great king? He had not been fair. Why did she think these people would be any different?

As if sensing her thoughts, Ren paused, evaluating her. The way his blue eyes appraised her, it seemed he was judging her worth as an equal, as an adversary. She held his stare, sensing that if she looked away his opinion of her would diminish. Another test.

His eyes not leaving hers, he said, "Your line begins anew this day. As the Fates saw fit for the Dark and Light, so too shall it be for your race. You will obey the laws of their nature, the ones set in place since the beginning of time, and you will be brought back into the fold as it should have been the day you were created."

Xali let out a breath of relief.

"Turn our back on our gods?" she heard Carnick's mother ask. Xali bristled, knowing the question was one best kept silent.

The brilliance of Ren's eyes dimmed, their hue softening to the blue of the night sky when the stars were lit, and the sun had just settled to sleep. Xali felt the Dark power as it slipped past her and sent her aunt crumbling.

"Mother," Carnick said, starting to go to her, but Ren held his hand up in a gesture to stop him. Carnick looked torn.

"I did not say I was finished. Interrupt me again, and you will not live to feel the pain."

His eyes were now an ebony that rivaled the king's. The magic faded, and Carnick relaxed as his mother slowly rose, his father putting a hand out to help her, one which she ignored in her pride. Xali, however, saw the shake in her legs and her hands as she straightened herself to standing.

"As punishment for the crimes your family has committed against us and our people, your powers will be stripped. The Fates have spoken, binding is too subtle, they will completely remove the power that has been warped by your indiscretions and greed."

No one spoke for fear of punishment, but Xali could feel the angst, the confusion, the desperation at his words. To take their power would be like taking a limb. She wondered absently what binding would have encompassed in comparison but knew not to ask.

The others remained quiet, too fearful to speak so Xali spoke for them. "The Fates made this decision?" Ren's eyes shifted to a deep blue as he looked upon her. "How is that even possible?" she continued before he had the chance to answer.

"My mother is favored by the Mother Fate."

He glanced back at the queen, and she gave him a beautiful smile, her eyes twinkling. With her smile, the heaviness of the room dissipated for just that moment. Xali still didn't understand what Ren meant, and as if he could read her thoughts, he turned back and continued talking.

"Your power will fade within a few moons, and by the eve of my ascension to the throne, it will be gone."

"When is that?"

"Six moons if we still follow the same timeline as the day Drakine stole everything from us."

This time, there was reaction, and Xali feared the consequences should they continue.

"Be quiet," she said in a hushed tone. They ignored her, and she caught Ren's eye again. He was waiting, evaluating her again. Testing, but why and for what reason? Was there more? She turned to her family, reaching down past her fear and grabbing her strength. "Quiet!" she commanded, causing them to all stop and look at her, their taken aback expressions bolstering her. "Stay quiet for your own sakes and let him finish."

She turned back, catching Carnick's eyes. He wasn't shocked; instead, his face was filled with pride. She held her head higher and faced Ren who seemed pleased with her response. He glanced back at his parents again and gave them a nod. She could have sworn they were talking to each other. What were they saying, were they discussing the fate of her family with every misstep they took in this room? Every interruption? Every mention of their gods?

"As reward for questioning, for seeing past the façade and waking us," he said, turning back to Xali, "that power will flow to Xali, who will take the throne and rule until her heir with Carnick takes it upon her death, and so it will be going forward."

Xali's jaw fell, and she heard Carnick mumble proudly, "I'll be damned."

Ren didn't give the family a chance to react, continuing. "Against my father's advice, your family will remain alive, and their lives are yours, Xali. The Fates have deemed there will be only one heir from your blood going forward just as there is with the other two higher powers. There will be no more offspring aside from your son and directly from his line going forward. No exceptions, no choice as was given to the Elvin. Your ancestors abused that choice, and it has been revoked."

"I don't understand," Xali said honestly.

"You are queen, Xali. You will be crowned by my parents within the moon. You will rule your people just as the Elvin king rules his. You will hold the power your forefathers once did and master the gifts your creators gave you so that the true magic of your line can be passed on as it was meant to be. You will redefine your house and your people, the first to rule as the Mother Fate and the Dark Fate first intended when you were created through their love. Carnick will rule alongside you, as reward for his faith in you, his power will remain as well. You, however, will be the true voice of your people, the leader they follow."

She didn't know what to say, her legs felt weak, her mind overwhelmed. Rule. As queen. The words didn't make sense.

"I…I can't rule. I'm a second born. Carnick should rule, not I—"

It was Carnick who answered. "You were meant for this, Xali. You've always been meant for more than a foolish label." He looked back angrily at their family as he said it. Bringing his eyes back to hers, he took her hands. The love he held for her poured from his eyes, and she gulped back the tears that threatened to spill.

"This is your destiny, Xaliandri. It has always been."

"But you were to be king," she whispered.

He laughed. "I will be king to your queen, by your side, Xali. This is your moment to change it all, to redefine who we are, and I will be by your side every moment of it."

His words touched her, her heart swelling in response. She smiled, pushing the tears back that were threatening to spill.

"Take them," Ren commanded and the men in black cloaks moved to her family. They were gone within seconds.

"No!" she yelled. "You said they would live!"

Ren raised his brow. "Did I?"

Her heart thumped in fear then his lip curved. "Still yourself. They will live. Be thankful my judgment favors my mother's blood, or they would all be dead by now."

Relief flooded her. Had he been making an attempt at play? It wasn't the type of play she appreciated, and she wanted to yell at him for scaring her so, but she refrained.

"Thank you for your mercy," Carnick said, as she pulled herself together.

"Where have you taken them?" she asked.

"Someplace safe while we discuss your rule," the king answered.

The men in white robes disappeared as the brother said, "I'm done with these formalities. I don't know how you stand this. Glad we won't have to put up with this again."

Xali caught the smile Ren held, one that made it appear as though he were holding back a laugh. So, there was a playful side to him. Perhaps his Dark side was the reason it had presented itself in such an uncomfortable fashion a few moments earlier.

"Go, Tynan. Take Paige and Chastity," the king said.

"I'm stuck with Paige? Isn't that Ren's job?"

The woman with the brown hair crossed her arms and shot him an annoyed look.

"I wouldn't get on her bad side, Uncle," Ren said. "She may look meek, but she's a spitfire."

Paige's blue eyes looked upon Ren with love, and Xali wondered at their relationship. What was it that had brought them together? She looked petite and soft in the presence of her husband, in the presence of any of the immortals in fact.

"Go, I shan't be long," Ren said to his wife.

The brother took them both, and Xali couldn't help but ask, "You can't speak to her in her mind?"

He eyed her, and she was unsure if he would answer her.

"You ask too many questions," the king said.

"It is my questions that found you," she replied before she could stop herself.

"She's right, Father. She deserves answers if she is to rule as my counterpart."

His father nodded.

"Paige and Chastity are not true immortals as you call us. They are neither Light nor Dark powered. In fact, they hold no magic."

Xali was confused, and her face must have reflected that confusion. They held no magic but were immortal. The way he had said it led her to believe they were anomalies, but why?

"There is much to our past that remains unknown to you. You will have time to discover it, but now is not that time," the king explained.

"Now," the queen said, "it is time for something more. Ren, bring Carnick, please."

"Yes, Mother."

The queen came forward, taking Xali's hand before she could react. The room disappeared, replaced within seconds by the holy lands, the sun's heat taking the chill from Xali's soul, one she hadn't realized had settled there.

"The holy lands?" Carnick asked.

"My brother has given it a few alternative names that are far from holy," the king said. "This land is an affront to my kingdom and everything we are. My wife and I disagree entirely on its fate."

"Which is why I hold the final decision," Ren said, "one which favors my mother's, much to my father's chagrin."

"One which will anger the Dark Fates," the king argued.

"The Mother Fate can be very persuasive," the queen rebutted.

"Sometimes, I wonder at the connection between you and her," the king said. "You know too much, Vi."

"We slept a long time, Sinow, and in that time, she came to me often. Revealing that of which we were unaware when Drakine stepped upon our shores."

"It would have been helpful if she'd been forthright before they decimated our kingdom."

"We've known the Fates long enough to know they have their reasons."

"Ones I never grasp. Why subject our people to this, Vi? Why the travesty that befell them, not to mention us? What purpose did any of it serve?"

Xali quietly observed them, afraid to interrupt, a voyeur on a relationship with which she was unfamiliar. As she watched the queen place her hand on his cheek, his eyes lightening to a rich brown, she saw not two immortals, only two people deeply in love.

She glanced at Ren who seemed accustomed to these interactions, his eyes surveying the holy lands.

"I have no answers as to why our people were made to suffer so nor why we endured so long without each other," the queen said, "delaying the ascension, delaying the inevitable. I do know it served a purpose."

She let her hand slowly drift from his cheek to his chest where it lingered briefly. There was an intensity to the moment, and Xali could feel the heat between them, the desire that lay under the calm exteriors.

"She is the purpose, the redemption for the sins of her people against the Mother Fate and against us," she continued.

The king gave a sigh sounding resigned to follow her lead whether he liked it or not, as if whatever it was she knew was beyond his comprehension, something unseen to which only she was privy.

"Damned instinct," he mumbled.

"You should be used to it by now," she replied, kissing his cheek.

He grumbled but said no more, and Xali noticed a slight shift in the color of his eyes, as close to what she would call a twinkle as there could be in someone so formidable. Xali drew her gaze away and looked out at the holy land. Carnick had walked a few steps away, his eyes on the shrine of the gods.

The queen came and stood next to her. "You are the change, the final step in a journey that has been long fraught with mistakes and lies but the first step on one that will correct the wrongs and forge a new path. You are the future of your people and your family, Xaliandri. Together, you and Carnick will lead them to become a greater people."

"And it all starts here," Ren finished.

"In the holy land?" she asked, her head once again overwhelmed.

"Yes, but to my husband's point, you will change the name." She walked toward the shrine of the gods, closer to where Carnick stood listening. "And this blasphemous thing."

"But our people worship our gods," Carnick said. "We always have."

"Your creators are the same as ours, your gods the same as we worship, simply called something different, and missing a few, I might add."

"We are not demanding your people worship any different than they have, only that it be acknowledged that the gods and the Fates are one," the king said. "Your people suffered the wrath of neglecting to remember this in the past."

"They did? But it's your people who have suffered not ours," Xali braved.

The king's eyes darkened as Ren turned his attention to her. She braced herself for punishment, but the queen spoke instead.

"Long before Drakine brought your people to our shores, your land flourished. It was rich with lush vegetation, crops that fed the entire land, plants like nothing we have on our shores."

Xali couldn't believe what she was hearing.

"No, Drakine brought us here because it was a wasteland, our homeland stolen from us," she said without thinking.

"Is that what you know to be true, Xali, or what we've been taught?" Carnick asked.

He was right, the lies were embedded so deeply it was hard to see past them.

"You are right on some counts, the truth has simply been distorted for you." The queen bent and picked up a handful of sand, letting the grains slip through her fingers as she continued. "This land was dying but not because of anything our people did. The Mother Fate cursed your land. You forgot her, created idols of men you believed to be your gods, writing her out of your history, and so your land suffered. Without her love, it died."

"The pride of your ancestors destroyed your lands. The Fates are vindictive when their path is not followed," the king said, looking at his wife. Something passed between the two that made Xali wonder at their history and what mistakes they had made.

"So why bring us here?" Carnick asked. "For a history lesson?"

The king's eyes grew a shade closer to black. "Don't make me regret acquiescing to my son's decision."

"You are here to understand where your people came from and where they are heading," Ren replied, stepping in. "This land is yours, it is land given to your ancestors by the Fates, regardless of the reason, regardless of the fact that your ancestors were forced away, it is still land where your people are meant to live."

Xali's heart dropped, they were banishing their people to dead lands. She began to argue, but the queen turned, the sand still sifting through her fingers.

"Your people will be relocated to the land of their creation, and we are taking our kingdom back," she said.

"But you can't do that. We'll die out here, the land is barren, there is no food, no water."

"Did not your people cast ours out to suffer?" the king asked as the queen moved away.

Xali held back her emotions and nodded.

"Watch," he said, gesturing to his wife.

Xali followed his eyes, drawing a breath as in the wake of each of the queen's footfalls sprung grass and flowers that spread out past her in rolling waves until the land was covered with glorious colors.

Carnick moved closer and put his hand around her waist as they watched in wonder, the world coming to life all around them. As the ground continued to transform, the queen turned, her eyes a striking emerald. With her turn, trees burst through the ground, saplings that grew to massive, towering structures. The land beneath them swelled, and Carnick clung to Xali, trying to hold her steady.

A rush of water was heard, and a spout burst forth, far in the distance. It flowed, snaking its way toward them as the ground changed to accommodate it. A river formed in its wake.

The wind whipped Xali's hair as the queen motioned her over. Moving to her side, she looked in wonder at the beauty of the land before her. Land that had once been her people's, one made so that they could flourish. This was what they had turned their back on in their obsessed hatred of the Fates, their own stubbornness and belief in the wrong deities had in some ways been a self-fulfilling prophecy. The further they'd strayed, the less the Mother Fate had favored them, the more they'd lost, and so the more they believed they'd been slighted in favor of the other races. In reality, it was their own doing that had cost them everything.

Taking in the flourishing land before her, she felt the connection, a sense that she was home, at one with it. A feeling she'd only come close to in one other place in the kingdom, and beyond the guardian wall. The land of the Elvin. But had that been her own feelings, or had it been her connection to the queen that had driven her reaction, that pull she'd had to the land of her ancestors? She opened herself to it and realized that had indeed been the case. This was different, unique to what she'd felt then. Her heart swelled, and a sob escaped. She was overcome with a feeling of contentment, of peace, of being. She was home.

"When I am away from Cirillia, I feel it deep in my core, like there is a part of me that is empty. It's an intense feeling, the same I have when I'm not by my husband's side. I imagine you've always had that feeling and never understood it was the call of your homeland."

Xali nodded, afraid to speak, knowing the tears would follow.

"I will leave the shrine to you. I think you know what needs to be done."

She walked away, leaving Xali to stare now at the shrine. Where before it had always seemed a peaceful, comforting space, well suited to its surroundings, now it appeared out of place, an atrocity to the beauty that lay around her.

Xali lifted her hand, letting nature call to her, listening for it as the Elvin king had taught her. She closed her eyes, giving herself over to the magic that stirred deep within, then sent it out in a wave toward the shrine. The magic crested within her just before she set it loose, and she knew then that this was her destiny, this was her path, just as the queen had said.

Carnick watched as the green speckles in Xali's eyes shifted to a bright emerald, his heart swelling with pride as she released her power. He'd taken it in, listening to all the immortals had said, all of it reaffirming his suspicions about her and her place in their world. The specialness he'd always seen in her.

As her power crashed upon the shrine, it morphed, vines climbing from below, flowers overrunning them as they wrapped their way through the structure. The living world overran it, the light curtains that blew in the breeze layered in flowers that appeared to melt into the fabric, leaving imprints he knew would never fade. Trees burrowed their way from below, their roots encasing the columns, blooming as they rose, the colors of her creations in shades unlike any in the other provinces. Kingdom, he corrected himself. This world had once been a kingdom, torn asunder by his family, now made whole by the woman he loved.

"She needs to hear the Dark magic, she favors the nature side too strongly," he heard Ren say.

"Sounds like someone else when he was young," his father replied.

"Aye, it does."

"And you, Carnick, need to recognize the nature, you heed the Dark too greatly."

"I don't know how to do that, this is what I've always known," he replied honestly.

"Which is why your family's magic is so destructive," the queen said. "With the two blended as they once were, your kind will do amazing things."

As she said it, Xali stopped the flow of her magic, stepping back to appraise her creation. She looked back at him, and he fell in love with her again. She was breathtaking, her eyes twinkled with emerald sparkles that danced in the storm clouds. Her hair played in the wind, her cheeks flushed with excitement. She'd always been the most attractive of the cousins, her beauty eclipsing theirs, but now she was exquisite, the events of the past few days transforming her to her full potential, the magic that she now embraced enhancing what had always been there. His heart brimmed with pride, the potential he'd always seen in her, the one no one else had seen, had finally been met, and the woman before him was the queen she'd always been meant to be.

She gestured for him to join her, and he looked first to the immortals, the king nodding his ascent. He walked to her and took the hand she had extended to him.

"I need your magic with mine," she said.

He looked at her questioningly.

"It feels right, there's something missing."

She turned from him to face the garden she'd created. He had no idea what she intended for him to do, so he followed her lead. Raising his hand as she had, he let his power flow, watching as it met hers, the two creating a brilliant blend of gray and green hues that danced along the garden. He felt the connection to her magic, and something within clawed to be noticed. He acknowledged it, slowly letting it free. It felt strange and uncomfortable, his usual magic straining against it, treating it like an enemy. He ignored the sensation, and as a slight gray mist escaped her hand, morphing with the green, so too a trickle of green hue fled its cage within him and met the gray hues of his own, the result a vivid stream of violet that rivaled the sun's brightness. Storm clouds developed, shutting out all light but their magic. The stone below the structure crumbled. The tree roots rose to take their place, leaves on the flowers darkening, rich shades of red, mauve, navy. The leaves drew closer to forest green, their depth astonishing. He stared at the transformation, his magic withdrawing with hers.

Both stood, too stunned to speak until finally, Xali said, "This is what we were meant to be. And who we now are."

He looked at her, the emerald sparkles in her eyes now interlaced with violet ones.

"You are going to make an amazing queen."

"And you will be an amazing king. We are equals, Carnick."

He pushed a lock of her hair back.

"No, Xali, you've never been anyone's equal. But together, we will rule this new land."

"It's beautiful, isn't it?" she said, looking out at their new world. "I feel like I'm home."

He knew exactly what she meant. Although he'd never realized he was anywhere but home, he now understood this was their true home. The sensation ran deep within him. He'd always felt at one with the holy land but never realized it went beyond the shrine of the gods. Shrine? The term didn't fit what now stood before him. This was more of a garden, a memorial of sorts to what he imagined must have been the Mother Fate. He still wasn't entirely sure who she was, but from all he'd heard, she was mother to his people, gentle, nature bound, and with a vengeful streak that had cost his people everything when they'd turned their back on her. It was odd to think they'd made the same mistake twice, and now they were losing it all again. Their royal line recreated, their land no longer theirs, forced to migrate to one only their ancestors had known. All because they had failed to recognize the truth, all because they had blamed the very Fate who had protected them.

"Now it's time for things to change," Xali said, bringing his attention back. She glanced over her shoulder at the immortals then raised her hand once more.

The wind whipped past Carnick, stirring his hair, its direction—the garden. His mouth dropped as the wind rushed against the stone etching deep within the former shrine. It was the one recognizable piece left, but it wouldn't be for long. The carvings quickly disappeared, the stone drifting away as sand might in a windstorm. Soon, there was nothing blocking his view through the garden to the land beyond.

The sand floated out of the structure, hanging in status before them. Xali dropped her hand and tilted her head, watching with them all as the grains moved, morphing into the shape of a woman. He could make out the long straight hair that danced in the wind, the graceful shape of her and the emeralds that glittered where her eyes would be. It floated there for only a moment before the wind took it away.

The air was still, and silence drifted upon it.

"Change," he repeated Xali's word, thinking on what it meant for them. An uneasy feeling settled within him.

Change, it was something their people hadn't done in ten thousand years. Something that suddenly filled him with an overwhelming sense of foreboding.

Two

Ren paced the room, his mind lost in thought so that he didn't hear Paige come upon him.

"You're worrying," she said, stopping his motion by insinuating her body into his path.

"I'm not worrying," he replied, giving her a kiss.

She wrapped her arms around his neck and peeked up at him, her eyes revealing the doubt in his words.

"You're fretting on something, Ren. I know that look."

"I don't fret."

"Yes, you do. Just as your father does. Sinow is the king of worry, and you are the prince of it."

"Did you come to harass me purposely?" he asked, raising a brow.

"No, I came to find out why you're pacing so loud that even the

Fates can hear you."

He sighed, pulling her hands from his neck and kissing them. Her bright blue eyes awaited an answer, and he'd been married to her long enough to know she wouldn't be deterred from getting one.

"I can't help but wonder if I did the right thing, made the right choice."

Her eyes grew serious.

"The girl? Xali?"

"Yes, my father, my uncle, they wanted her punished, all of them."

"And what did my husband want?"

"I don't know, Paige. My Dark side wants them gone, given due justice for disrupting our lives, slaughtering our people. But the other two sides say different."

"What does your instinct say?"

"I can't rule on instinct."

"Your mother does, and it has served her well for eons. It is only when she questions her instinct that there have been consequences."

"You sound like your father."

"My father is a wise man."

He began to pace again. "My instinct tells me she's important. That she has a place, that she is meant to rule her people. The sins of the father shall not be borne by his children."

"Then you have your answer."

He stopped pacing, letting his doubts fade and listening to his instinct, listening for anything that led him to believe this had been the wrong choice. Then, he ran his hand through his hair as she lay a hand on his chest.

"Still the worry?"

"More like a sense of something. That this isn't where it ends."

"It's not. Their kingdom needs to be built, their people resettled."

"Our kingdoms healed."

"Rebuilt," she continued. "This is only the beginning."

"That's what concerns me."

"The unknown, and Dark kings despise the unknown," she said with a wink, her lips curving to a smile that lit her face. Although they'd been asleep for the duration, the idea of having been away from that smile, from her for so long was devastating, and it angered the Dark and Elvin blood within him. Ten thousand years seemed an endless time to have been without her.

"You know me too well, Paige."

"It's my job to know you well. How else am I to sit on that throne beside you?"

He knew she was teasing him, but her words cut at the other worry within him. One which had been growing prior to all of this, prior to their endless sleep.

"And there it is again," she said, her fingers tracing his furrowed brow again. "It's not simply Xali and her people, is it, Ren?"

He lowered his eyes, but her fingers dropped to pick his chin up, forcing him to look at her.

"Ren?"

"No, it's not," he answered.

"Violissa and Sinow?"

He nodded, knowing his emotions were tenuous, and if he spoke of his parents, his Dark side would rebel at the softness in his heart, the Light wanting to embrace it.

"They'll be all right. They're ready, Ren."

"Are they? They've been separated again for ten thousand years. Now, they've reunited only to be torn apart for eternity."

"The rules of ascension are clear, Ren, the reigning king must return to the Fates as the incoming king ascends. It's unavoidable, and I thought you'd come to terms with it."

"I had before millennia were stolen from us, from them."

She studied him and sighed. "They'll be all right. None of us truly knows what will happen to them. They might end up together."

He cocked his brow. "You don't really believe that, do you?"

Her face grew sad. "I have to believe it because the alternative is heartbreaking. If I don't believe it, I don't know how I'll say good-bye to them. And then to my father."

Paige's father was a Lightbearer, the only immortal outside the royal line to bear a child. She was a gift from the Fates, and Ren was grateful every day that she was here.

He pulled her in against his chest, holding her tight and kissing her head. "He'll be all right, perhaps he'll even find your mother's spirit."

Their moment of solitude was severed when his uncle shifted into the room. Paige jumped at his sudden appearance, but Ren shot him an angry look, letting Paige go.

"Do you ever knock, Tynan?" he growled at his uncle.

"A question your father has asked me for lifetimes and one to which I happily reply no."

"Why are you here?"

"I see I've interrupted a moment, should I return later?" he said sarcastically.

"Too late now," Paige muttered.

Tynan laughed. "Your mother wishes to speak to you."

"And why didn't she call me herself?"

"Because I wanted a word with you first."

"Tynan, we have little time before—"

"I know, I won't take but a moment."

Ren looked at Paige who shrugged and said, "I know when I'm not wanted. I will leave and let you do your big boy talk."

She kissed him on the cheek and then nodded to Tynan on her way out.

Ren crossed his arms over his chest.

"Always so guarded yet your worry can be felt throughout the keep."

That surprised Ren.

"You worry as your father does. It casts a fog around the keep."

"I doubt that very much. What is it you want, Uncle?"

"To see if you worry that your decision was too rash? Having doubts? Or…is it your parents' fate that torments you so."

"Will you be returning to the Fates with them or staying on to vex me?" he quipped.

Tynan laughed. "Ah, I do love to irritate you, nephew. In truth, I have yet to decide. It has been a long life, but the thought of nights without Chastity to warm my bed seems a tad torturous, especially after ten thousand years without her touch."

"Perhaps she'll remain with you?"

"You know as well as I how it works. We are spirits wandering the world or the skies for eternity. Not much of a blessing if you ask me. An eternity in ephemeral form? Why is that the Fate of our kind?"

The tension returned to Ren.

"Ah, so it is your parents that are on your mind."

"A little of both, I suppose."

"Well, you know my opinion on the girl. She should have been killed along with the whole lot of them. They're a scourge on our kingdom. One your father and I questioned when their kind stepped foot on our land. You and your mother with your soft hearts took them in and look what happened."

His words should have angered Ren, but instead, they gave him pause.

"Why didn't Mother's instinct warn her? Why was she driven to take them in as guests rather than have them turned away when they reached our shores?"

Tynan looked befuddled. "I don't know. Your mother's instinct is always keen to sense things that we don't. It's very perplexing."

"The only explanation I have is that this was meant to happen," Ren said.

"All of it? The near decimation of the three races at the hands of theirs?"

"Yes." He began to pace as he thought it through.

"A means to an end," Tynan said before Ren could. "That's what your mother says about every tragedy. But to what end?"

"Xali."

"The girl?"

"Yes. Their people were abandoned, their power diluted—"

"Where it should remain."

"No, this is Xali's path. It always has been. Just as prophecy has driven our family…" He stopped, unsure of his thought, or the impact it would have if spoken aloud.

"It has driven theirs," Tynan finished.

He nodded. "If the Fates created my parents' prophecy to right the wrongs from their past, so they may have written one to right the wrongs that caused the abandonment of Xali's people."

"Or perhaps it's intertwined with the same prophecy that has ruled your parents."

Those last words hung in the air, neither knowing what to say. To think that the prophecy wasn't completed, that a piece they'd never known existed, still lingered to be resolved was a stunning revelation and one that changed everything they knew about the prophecy.

Three

Carnick watched from the doorway as Xali struggled once again with the gown that challenged her usual sense of fashion.

"I do believe you've finally been bested," he said, laughing.

She turned, her lips pouting, her beauty entrancing. Her hair was up, braids laying throughout that then piled atop her head in an elegant form, small diamonds strategically placed within it, catching the light that flooded the room. Her eyes were set against a dark makeup that she rarely wore, the emerald flecks dazzling against the gray that held them, her lips a deep red, stained by the berries grown in the southern province.

She was adorned in a gown befitting a queen, the loose style falling past her feet and draping across the floor behind her, the blue of their houses bringing out the silver of her locks, the few stray strands along her exposed neck calling to him. The gown fell from her shoulders, the neck dropping just so the curve of her breasts could be seen, then collapsing down her back to reveal the lush ivory skin that graced her back.

He couldn't take his eyes from her.

"That bad?" she asked, her brow creasing.

Catching his breath, he laughed. "Terrible."

Her face dropped.

"Because there's no way that I'll be able to focus with you looking like this."

Her tension faded as he took her in his arms.

"You are exquisite, my dear."

A blush filled her cheeks.

"And you hate every minute of this, don't you?" he teased.

She smiled. "Up until you arrived."

He kissed her, tasting the berry and wondering if it had been a good idea to kiss her, not certain he could resist removing her dress.

She pulled back and cocked her brow as though reading his thoughts.

"It took me too long to get made up like this for you to undo it all."

He couldn't help but laugh. Kissing her nose, he let her go and stood back.

"You know, you look quite handsome yourself," she said, running her fingers down the navy surcoat he'd worn atop the embellished tunic that reflected the status of his house. It was something he rarely wore as he preferred his everyday clothes, the comfort of them. This was constricting, the jacket running past his waist and tapering almost to his knees. With gold embroidery tracing the seams and the cuffs of his arms in the sigil of his house, it spoke of his rank as a royal, something he'd always preferred not to make so obvious, unlike other members of his family.

"Must be a special occasion to get you in this outfit," she said playfully.

"Yes, the same that forced you into this one."

She threw her head back and laughed, her graceful neck exposed. He had the urge to kiss it when he heard a familiar voice.

"Pardon the intrusion."

Carnick moved away from Xali quickly as her mother stepped into the room. She raised her brow at Carnick, and for a moment, he wondered if she would chastise him for touching her daughter before they were joined.

"I suppose all traditions are now lost," she said softly. There was a sadness in her eyes for a moment then a resolve. "They were kind enough to let us remove our treasures from our palaces before they tore them down." Her voice quivered.

The heaviness of the occasion returned, the reality that he'd escaped for those few minutes crashing down upon him again. The immortals had given him and Xali temporary shelter in what they called their southern home. Letting their family stay with them while they took back their world. The family palaces had all been demolished, any sign of their rule wiped away. The palaces of the immortals, or castles as they were called, had been rebuilt with magic and now four of them stood where before there had only been ruins. Their people would be resettled next but not until Xali was crowned. For the time being, they were allowed to remain in the kingdom as the people of the immortals slowly took back the land that had once belonged to their ancestors. There had been several uprisings, their people confused, scared, not understanding why what had been theirs and their family's before this was being ripped from them. It would take a strong ruler to settle them, to help them see the truth behind the lies they'd been fed for generations, to help them accept their new lives. Carnick had no doubt Xali was that ruler; she was an unwilling queen whose strength went beyond what the surface reflected.

He knew it would be an uphill battle, one for which he wasn't certain she was ready, but he would be there by her side. Even if the rest of the family turned their back on her, something they'd already begun to do.

Nothing was as it had been, all now stripped from them. Half the family wouldn't even acknowledge them; his mother hadn't spoken to him since their sentencing. It had been a moon cycle, and she refused to be in the same room as him still.

"I thought you should have these," Xali's mother said, halting Carnick's thoughts. "They were given to me by my mother. Each daughter is handed down the jewels of her mother at her crowning or her betrothal. I suppose as this will be both occasions for you, it's only right that you have them today."

It was then he noticed the gray box in her hands. He watched as Xali opened the box. A glorious gem lay within a soft cushion of gray, attached to a thick silver necklace. Smaller blue gems made their way up each side of it surrounded by tiny diamonds. In the center sat a bracelet with the same gems, one that would wrap delicately around her wrist, then run up her forearm as was the style of their people.

Xali's mother took the necklace and placed it on Xali's neck. It sat perfectly against her ivory skin.

"You look beautiful, Xaliandri."

"Thank you, Mother."

She helped her with the bracelet then kissed Xali's cheek before rushing from the room. With her fled the lightness of their prior mood. Xali fingered the gem, her hand shaking. Carnick met her eyes, and in them, he saw the broken woman she'd been trying to hide. The one who blamed herself for the fall of her family, who took every insult she heard whispered to heart, who could never go back even if she wanted to.

He moved to her and took her hands. "Stop," he said. "Do not doubt yourself."

"How can I not?"

"Because you did the right thing, Xali. You did what no one else was ever brave enough to do."

"I destroyed us, and they will forever hate me for it."

"So what if they do? When have you ever worried what others think or say about you?"

Her eyes searched his, the tears sparkling behind them.

"No, you can't break, Xali. You've come too far. This is your destiny now, not the family's, not the great king's, not mine. It's yours, and you can grab it and show them all the woman I know you to be, or you can run from it and validate their thoughts. The woman I know would take it and make it hers."

"You called me a woman. You've always called me a girl."

"So, I did. You are about to be crowned queen of a new land, you are about to become my wife, I think that makes you a woman."

"I thought you made me a woman that night we shared your bed for the first time," she said shyly.

He couldn't help but smile. "That too."

She reached up and kissed him.

"That will be enough of that," his mother's stern voice broke through the moment, causing them to jump. If she'd heard what they'd said, she didn't make mention of it.

"Mother," he said, unable to hide the edge in his voice.

"No matter what your mother thinks, Xaliandri, there are still traditions that should be kept in place. One of those is to remain chaste until you are joined."

"We're joining today, Mother."

"And I'm no longer chaste," Xali said, crossing her arms and staring his mother down.

What is she doing? Carnick thought as he gave her a side glance.

His mother eyed him then looked back at Xali who never averted her eyes.

"You do have spirit, child, there is no doubt in that. Never did act like you were a second born, but I suppose you never really were, were you? Don't let your father find out. I do hope it was my son and not one of those mongrel immortals."

"Mother!"

Xali's cheeks filled with her blush.

"Good. Now as much as you enjoy ignoring traditions, there is one we will keep." She placed a small pair of ear cuffs in Xali's hand. They were adorned with the same small blue and diamond gems that the necklace and bracelet held.

Xali stared at them.

"Here," his mother said, taking one of them. She fitted each to the outside of Xali's ears as she spoke. "It is tradition for the mother to hand her jewels over and for the mother of the betrothed to gift something to the bride. These were given to me on the day of my joining, and it seems right to pass them now to you." She stood back and admired the pieces. "You truly do hold the most beauty of any of us, don't you?"

"Thank you," Xali said softly. "They're beautiful." She gently fingered the jewels that now decorated her ears from the top curve down to the lobe.

His mother's stern look returned. "Carnick, I wish to speak with you alone if I can pull your hands from your betrothed for a few moments."

He nodded, then kissed Xali's cheek before quickly following his mother out of the room. He took one last look back at Xali and mouthed, "I shan't be long."

Catching up with his mother, he walked silently beside her, glancing at her in an attempt to read her mood. She looked tired, her hundred and twenty years showing. His mother had always been strong, fierce some would say. She was the strength of the family. It hurt him to see her this way, but then he thought of how she'd avoided him these last few days, and the anger returned.

She stopped in front of a window that looked out into a thick grove of trees. It seemed an odd place for a castle, nestled within the trees, sitting upon the only piece of open land within the grove, situated far to the south from the other lands. He wondered briefly at the significance of the placement until his mother began to speak.

"Your father and I have agreed to attend your nuptials today."

"And Xali's crowning?"

She tensed, her lips forming a sour expression.

"Yes, the immortal woman is not only quite alluring, but she is also quite persuasive. A few of us will attend, Xali's parents, your sister, and her brother as well as a few of your cousins. The others refuse to acknowledge her."

"And you? Will you acknowledge her?"

She turned sharply, her eyes a wave of storm clouds that threatened to cast their power upon him. He straightened to his full height, towering over her petite frame.

"What she has done…what you have allowed her to do has destroyed us all."

"What I allowed her to do? Xali makes her own decisions, Mother."

"She is a second born!" she snapped. "You a first born! You make the decisions, she obeys. It is her place to heed your command."

He studied her. "Birth order means nothing, Mother."

"It means everything to us."

"Because one man deemed it to be so eons ago. Why is Xali any less than me? Father any less than you? Only because words written by a deceiver tell us so. The same deceiver who told us this land was ours, that the immortals were weak. I assure you they are far from it."

"You will concede your right to rule to her?"

"Xali will rule, and I will be by her side as she does."

"You buck tradition, both of you, yet you will still take her as your wife? After all she has done, you will join with her? Why not throw that to the wind as well? You defy our laws so much, what is one more tradition to break?"

"I love her, Mother."

"Love? Love has no place in our marriages. We marry for control, for power, to maintain the throne."

"Well, you've lost the throne, all of it. There is no longer any law that says I must marry Xali. I will marry her because I love her, and she loves me."

"You were always infatuated with that girl. Always protecting her, teaching her to play with swords."

"I didn't protect her, I taught her to protect herself, to learn to fight for herself."

"Perhaps you taught her too well."

With that she walked away, leaving him to contemplate her words, that guilt she wielded like a weapon plaguing him.

He stared out the window. How were they to carry forward with the family against them? Could they leave those who chose to deny change, to cling to the past, leave them behind? Would his mother be one of them, severing ties with him as punishment for what Xali and he had done? He dropped his head, his eyes vacantly falling to stare at the stone floor. He feared the future, the unknown of it, feared for Xali, for her safety.

He shook it off, knowing he needed to be strong for her then turned and walked back to her, leaving the shadow of his mother and the past behind.

Xali paced the room, wringing her hands until Carnick returned. His eyes were stormy, his frame tense, and she wondered what his mother had said.

"Not all of the family will attend your crowning."

Her heart sank. She'd expected it, but it still hurt. Her nerves returned, the doubt nearly knocking her over.

"Hey," Carnick said, lifting her chin. "We knew this would happen. The family is divided. Because of us, their power will fade, they have lost their houses, they have lost everything."

"That's not helping, Carnick."

"I know, but it's the truth. We will never be the same, there's no going back. Even if we could, would you?"

She thought about it. Life had been simple then, her path clearly defined as a second born. She would have married Carnick, born him children, and sat in her place by his side. It would have been easy. But easy was boring. She thought of the king and queen, the kiss they'd shared when she'd awakened, the passion it held. They would still be asleep, all of them, had she taken the easy route. Her destiny, missed.

"Easy but not right," she mumbled, bringing her eyes back up to his. "No, I would still have taken this path."

He smiled. "Then stop doubting yourself."

There was a knock at the door, and a handsome man with auburn hair and bright blue eyes entered.

"It is time," he said.

She looked at Carnick, butterflies running rampant through her body.

"This is your day, Xali."

She nodded, saying, "I'm ready," and praying she could make herself believe those words.

The man shifted them to a hallway and told them to wait outside two great doors before disappearing. Something told her they were no longer in the same castle; there was a feel to this space that she hadn't felt in the other. She walked to the doors, tracing her fingers over the ornamental gold etching that bordered it then onto the carving of vines and flowers stained as if real flowers had left their imprint. It reminded her of the Elvin castle in which she'd stayed when she'd run away. Were they in the enclave, or close to it?

Her attention was pulled away when several men shifted with their family, at least part of her family. Her father nodded to her, her mother staying close, Mendol and the other cousins keeping their distance, Carnick's mother blocking them, his father to her side.

The doors opened, and Xali turned back around to see an expansive garden of flowers in sizes and colors that rivaled the rest of the kingdom.

"Only these two have been summoned, the rest will wait until you are called" the auburn-haired man said, gesturing for Xali and

Carnick to enter.

The doors slammed behind her, silencing the rush of complaints.

Creatures flitted within the garden, ones she'd never seen, the hues on their bodies bold and rich. A fountain sat to the side, green water splashing playfully as she and Carnick walked through. The garden was open, the only full wall being where it was attached to the castle. A half-wall to the far left was covered in ivy and white blooms. Ahead of her, the garden stretched out into the open, where a colorful meadow stood, inviting one to continue forward. She looked up, noticing the mid-day sun was shaded upon them, branches from trees she could not see, covering them partially, ones overwhelmed with pink and white blooms, small streams of sunlight peeking through in places.

As she cast her eyes back down, she spied the queen near a robust bush of purple blooms.

"Thank you, Cody," the queen said with a gentle smile, one filled with love. He winked at her and then disappeared. Xali wondered what their relationship was. There were so many immortals in their circle, how were they all connected? The queen crossed the room, beckoning for them to come close. She seemed to glide gracefully, the flowers leaning to her as she moved by them. Her emerald eyes shimmered in the sunlight.

Xali didn't know whether to bow or stay as she was. The mere presence of the queen left her awestruck. She could feel the woman's power as it cascaded through the room, a gentle blanket that calmed the soul. There was a lovely lilac scent that Xali now realized she'd noticed each time she'd been in the queen's presence.

"Where are we?" Carnick asked, breaking her trance.

"We are in our northern home. It was once my parents' home, the garden once my mother's," she replied, taking Xali's hand and leading her away. "This castle was once home to the Elvin. When Sinow's grandfather waged war with the realms, they fled to the enclave, gifting the castle to my father's line. It sat as protection against the Dark forces that dared enter the Sacred Groves. But that is a history long forgotten, erased by Drakine, your ancestor, long ago."

Xali looked out to where the queen looked. A forest lay behind the meadow, but at the edge of the clearing lay a path that wound down and out of sight. The enclave lay beyond. That was the pull she'd felt when they'd arrived. She remembered the story Narilen, king of the Elvin had told her during her stay, the story of the sun and moon castles. This was the sun castle, the moon castle lying below in the valley where the Elvin Enclave lie. Xali turned, taking in the garden once again, the half-walls of stone that lined one side, the edge that met the castle, vegetation climbing the high walls, the vines that encapsulated all but the doorway from which they'd entered.

"The ruins," she said softly. "Carnick, we walked by here when the creature took us to the enclave that night when we found the stones. This was where the ruins sat."

Carnick's eyes grew wide with disbelief.

"My husband and I call this home most of the time. It sits directly between the three realms, deep within the Sacred Groves. It balances our powers. One day soon, it will be Ren's home," the queen continued like she hadn't heard Xali's revelation. She had a faraway look like she was seeing something that wasn't there for Xali to see, her eyes growing sad. "He will need that balance as will you both. Your path will not be easy, Xaliandri. You will be faced with challenges, some of which may seem impossible to conquer."

Carnick took Xali's hands as the queen's words sent a chill through her. She'd wanted to hear more about the past, to know what the Sacred Groves were and how the castle balanced their power, not quite understanding why that would be, but those last words stopped her, their weight a burden she wasn't certain she wanted to carry.

The queen turned to her, continuing, "Do not waiver from your path, no matter the temptation. It will cost you gravely, as it once did me."

"What happened to you?" Xali whispered, fearful to ask but too curious not to.

"The Fates can be cruel," she said softly, her eyes morphing to a deep sage, "but this is your story, it is no longer mine." Her eyes drifted to Carnick. "Stand by her, she will need your loyalty, your strength. They will come with a price, but that price must be met for our world to finally be one."

She moved from them, with a floating motion. Xali watched her, her heart pounding loudly. She glanced at Carnick, his brows knitted with concern, his grip tightening on her hand anticipating a threat that was yet to be present.

"It is time," the queen said as though she had not said any of the previous words.

Ren shifted with the auburn-haired woman by his side. The Dark king appeared, followed by his brother and Chastity. He took the queen in his arms, kissing her deeply like they'd been separated again for eons. Xali could feel the heat of it and remembered the story of how their love was bound by prophecy. He studied her, his fingers moving to a stray curl that hung on her cheek. It was a tender moment, one she felt should be theirs alone, and so she averted her eyes.

"Are you two going to be like this up until Ren's ascension?" the brother asked.

"They're always like this, Uncle," Ren answered.

"Did anyone else notice we have company?" Chastity asked.

The king shifted his gaze to Xali and Carnick, the softness of his eyes transforming as night overtook them. "So we do. Violissa, do you think that wise?"

"Sinow, we talked about this. Ren's decision stands."

He looked toward Ren. "It doesn't mean I trust them."

The woman with the auburn hair came toward them, her bright blue eyes shining happily.

"Paige," the king said, his voice holding the edge of a command.

"I haven't met them yet, and as they will be part of my life now,

I will say hello, Sinow."

"She's gotten quite bold since we returned, Sinow," the brother teased.

"She's been that way, Tynan, much to my displeasure."

She turned quickly, and Xali thought she caught a playful wink.

"You can't help but love her though, Father," Ren said, laughing.

"I don't have to love her, you do. I have to tolerate her as I've done for too many millennia," he responded, crossing his arms.

She had turned back to Xali and Carnick, a smile on her face. "He really does love me, whether he admits it or not," she whispered.

"I heard that, Paige."

Ignoring him, she continued, "I'm Paige, and since you will be stuck with me, as Sinow says, for your lifetime, I wanted to introduce myself."

"You're the princess?" Xali asked.

"Ha! She wishes," the brother said.

Paige rolled her eyes. "I am not part of the royal line. Nor would I want to be. But as I will be queen when Ren is crowned, I thought I should say hello."

"Hi," Xali said awkwardly.

Paige laughed, her eyes sparkling. "You are quite the beauty, aren't you," she said, "and you are strikingly handsome. Silver hair, and those eyes, it's like mini storms within each." She shook her head and walked back toward the others, neither Xali nor Carnick knowing how to respond. "Why is it the Fates bless all of you with unique beauty. I mean, I constantly feel like the plain one with you lot."

"Chastity's not one of us. She's plain, too," the king said, and Xali thought she could detect a playful tone.

Chastity put her hands on her hips. "Are you going to let him insult me?"

"Not picking a fight here, dear," the brother said. "Violissa will have my head if I mess up her gardens."

"What is going on?" Carnick whispered to Xali.

"I think we're getting a glimpse into what immortals are really like."

"Just like us?"

She nodded. "Exactly."

"Enough," the king said, his voice growing formal. "Tynan call the Councils, let's get this done."

He looked at Xali, his eyes which had turned a rich brown, growing black again. A black cloak appeared over him, and he drew the hood. Cloaks appeared on the others as well, only the king and his brother drawing their hoods.

Xali noticed the capes were different shades. Ren and Paige wore gray as did Chastity. The queen wore a glorious white cape with thick purple and pink flowers embroidered along the bottom and green stems and leaves flourishing it.

As the king's and queen's men appeared around the garden, a crown formed on the queen's head. It was silver with cerulean blue and emerald gems. The gems fell in places that were shaped as flowers, the flowers all interlacing as they made their way around the crown. Real flowers began to fill her hair, laying delicately within the curls. She was breathtaking, and Xali wondered if this was what the Fates themselves looked like.

"See," Paige said, "you just can't compete with that."

"I concede, Paige. I suppose I'll keep you company in that plain club," Chastity said, and Xali wondered what a club was other than something she'd seen used to give blows to unruly citizens.

A pink flush filled the queen's cheeks as the king's voice boomed.

"Bring in the witnesses, keep them far from my presence, or I won't hesitate to kill any one of them."

Xali's heart pounded, reality slamming back, the lightheartedness of the prior moments gone. She took them in. Ren, Paige, the brother, and Chastity had all moved back, leaving the king and queen in the forefront, commanding attention. The king, even without his face showing, looked intimidating, his stature overtaking the queen's. She herself tall and proud. His presence overpowered all else, the contrast of it against the calm of the gardens not lost on her.

Her family was brought in, standing behind them but with a slight distance that ensured a differentiation between them and Xali. Once they were settled, everyone waited. The room was quiet, even nature too terrified to speak.

The queen came forward. "We will hold your union first then once joined, you will be crowned. As I understand it, the joining ceremony for your people is unique to ours. Out of respect to your culture, one of your own will perform it, all of us standing witness to your vows."

She nodded toward their family. Xali and Carnick looked back as Xali's father came forward. He made his way to them quietly, the queen returning to her place next to her husband. Xali met her father's eyes, they were soft, lined with worry and weariness. He hesitated for a moment then began.

As he spoke the words, and they went through the motions, Xali's mind wandered. Joinings were celebratory, a time for the family to gather and celebrate, an event that lasted days with preparations and small ceremonies that took place prior to the final joining. This was nothing like it should have been. This was grim, overcast with fear and disappointment, trepidation. She wondered what it meant for her future with Carnick. Was it an omen, a forewarning of the trials that stood before them?

"Xaliandri," her father's voice pulled her from her thoughts, "do you accept Carnick's hand as he has accepted yours?"

"Yes," she answered quickly, feeling Carnick relax next to her.

"Then you are now joined as one, may the blessing of the gods be upon your journey together."

Fates, she thought, seeing the cringe on the queen's face. The gods did not exist; the Fates were the true gods. Xali looked down at the ribbons that now lined her arm. The blue and gold of Carnick's house crossing with the blue and silver of her own. As a second born, she was tied to both houses, the crossing of the ribbons symbolic of her duty to stay subservient to each, to obey her first-born husband who was free of the binds, having never born the constrictions of that of a second born.

Her father gave her a kiss on the cheek, a moment of softness, then he walked away. Xali held her arm out, staring at the bindings. She looked to the queen and king, equals to each other, no bindings to designate birth orders, both seen as one.

Carnick took her hand, bringing her arm toward him. He met her eyes. "I think it's time we leave some of our traditions behind," he said, "and begin our own." He turned her arm over and broke the binding, the ribbons falling to the floor. Something about the way they slowly fell gave her pause, a feeling she thought she should heed, a foreboding of sorts, but she pushed it aside. What he'd done had never been done, and the statement it made was not lost on her nor the family. He had freed her binds and in doing so had empowered her, bringing her to the status of a first born. That one small act established their path moving forward as equals.

He smiled, and her heart felt as though it would burst. "I've been waiting a long time to do that," he said as tears filled her eyes.

She tuned out the murmurs of shock from their family and kissed him.

"Can we get on with the crowning now." She heard the brother say. "This mushy stuff annoys me. Keep me here much longer, brother, and I will start killing mortals."

Xali pulled from Carnick's arms, laughing.

"That sounds like a great idea," he whispered.

She raised her brow. "Him killing us?"

He joined her laugh. "No, your crowning."

"Agreed. Let's get this done," the king said, instantly erasing the joy of the moment.

Carnick watched as the cheer in Xali's eyes morphed at the king's words. This entire day had been a whirlwind of emotion for them both, and he had a nudging feeling that this was only the beginning. The queen's words were ingrained in his head, *your path will not be easy.* The words she'd told Xali had sent fear through his heart. Now they were finally joined, and he should have been happy, it was the day he'd awaited, but it lie shadowed beneath the reality that their lives had been irrevocably changed the moment Xali had been pulled onto this path. One from which she could now not stray, or she would suffer as the queen had. He didn't know what had happened to the queen, but it had scarred her enough to warn Xali.

He studied the king. Had he feared for his wife? Had that fear taken hold of everything he was? He met Carnick's eyes, pulling his hood down, his bold stare an acknowledgment to Carnick's thoughts. Carnick envied him. He was confident, lacking any sign of fear. Even when they'd been searching for his wife, it had never shown. Carnick stood taller, feeling the call of whatever connection he had to the king's power. The Darkness.

"Xaliandri, Carnick, please step forward," the queen said. They moved away from the spot where they'd been joined, further from their family and closer to the immortals. Carnick didn't miss the significance of the request. A welcome into their fold, a separation from their past, a step toward their future.

The brother dropped a basket on the floor, the sound echoing through the quiet space, and walked away grumbling. Carnick couldn't take his eyes from the contents. Xali grabbed his arm, recognizing what he had. Out of it rose the crowns of each house. Only the head, the first born was ever crowned and so four crowns hung in the air before them. A stream of Dark power, an ebony tendril fled the king's hand and engulfed the crowns. The queen raised her hand, and Carnick watched as an emerald magic joined the king's, Dark and nature. The two powers danced as the crowns morphed, merging to become two, then shifting form, the two almost identical aside from their size. Onyx made up the foundation, the connecting patterns tracing the sigils of both their houses then cresting in spots to add the embellishments of the other two houses. All four now in two crowns. Navy gems emerged, sparkling within the stream of magic to perch along the points of each loop.

The magic faded, and Carnick let out the breath he was holding, hearing Xali do the same, her hand still tightly gripped on his arm. The crowns hung before them, the king and queen each taking one.

"Wearing the crown is a serious endeavor. You must lead your people with the morals of the Fates themselves. Your people have none before you who have followed that steadfast rule. Just as there are those in my line who abused that power, so your line has abused it," the king said. "Do you accept the responsibility, the power that comes with the crown, Xaliandri?"

"I…I honestly don't know. This isn't my path, it wasn't mine, ever, I never wanted to be queen." Her words tumbled out, and Carnick feared the king's reaction.

"Yet here you are. The hesitation you hold leads me to believe my wife is correct, and you will be exactly the ruler your people and their new land need."

He placed the crown on Xali's head. "Wear it bravely."

Carnick noted the choice of the word bravely and not proudly.

"And Carnick, you will sit at her side. Do you accept the role? To support her, to rule with her knowing her will is the final in your realm, that you may advise her but never manipulate her. Do you promise to be her strength, her most loyal defender, no matter the cost?" the queen asked.

"Yes, always."

She placed the crown upon his head, both the physical and figurative weight of it present.

"There are two crowns, but there will be only one heir, as the Fates have deemed it so," the queen said. "Only the Elvin, as I have said, may forfeit that restriction going forward, they being of lesser power. Never will there be a second child born to your line, your magic no longer diluted as it has been in the past. You will bear either daughter or son, Xaliandri, the Mother Fate has not spoken as to which is favored. If you bear a daughter, she will wear your crown, a son, he will bear Carnick's as it will be from that day forward."

Only one heir? Carnick had hoped for the two their family had always been blessed with, but the Fates had spoken. Who were they to defy the Fates now that their gods had been proven false? An entire lifetime worshipping the gods made it hard to imagine them as anything but real, hard to replace them so easily with Fates who were reshaping their lives with every step closer they came to an unanticipated future and further from a past of lies. There was something about accepting them that seemed more difficult to him than it did to Xali, and he wondered why that was.

"You will have domain over your people and over your land, but know this," the king said, interrupting Carnick's thoughts, "my law is final and obsolete. No matter that you lead your people every day. My law will be obeyed. I rule above you. There are no exceptions, and as it is so, it shall be with my son and his heir. Your people will be taught our ways or risk the consequences of punishment."

"I don't understand," Xali said.

"My laws stand above your laws, above your reign, above your word. I am the final justice in this land no matter the domain you are granted. The Elvin understand this just as you must. There will be no crimes unpunished, no plots uncovered, no deceit undiscovered. Punishment is swift and just. The heaviest of crimes exacting the heaviest of punishments."

"Death?" Carnick asked.

"Yes, by my Council's hands or mine. We do not tolerate law-breakers in our world."

"But how would you even know?" he asked.

The king gave an unsettling smile. "We know all, we are connected to any whose blood originates from the Dark Fates as yours does. My son hears the call of both sides of your blood. You, your family, your people. Be sure they know this, there will be no exceptions, no begging forgiveness. I will give you six moon cycles to prepare them, teach them, or their blood will be on your hands."

Carnick was trying to wrap his head around how that could even be when the king turned away.

"Then how did Drakine get past you?" Xali asked softly.

Damn her curiosity. The room grew still, the tension palpable, the queen's eyes becoming wide with surprise. Carnick could feel the Dark power that now cloaked the room; it was coming from the king, his brother, even the son whose blue eyes were now a deep black.

"Xali," Carnick whispered, pulling her back, trying to move her behind him as the king turned slowly around.

"You would be wise to silence your curiosity, or there will be no chance of an heir for your line. Drakine's name is now banned from this land on penalty of death at my hands."

He disappeared, leaving them all too stunned to move.

"Take them back," the son commanded before he too disappeared, taking his wife with him, the brother leaving at the same time with his mate.

The queen looked sadly at Xali as their family was taken away. She put her hand up to stay a cloaked man coming toward them then said, "My husband does not like to be questioned, nor does my son. He tolerates your presence with anger at the decision my son and I made to keep you alive, to let you rule your people alongside my son. Do not let your curiosity ruin that fragile trust he has with our sway. One cannot stop a Dark king from bringing justice, and he will kill you if given the opportunity as punishment for your family's crimes."

"I'm sorry. I only—"

"I know, but you have to remember Drakine bested us. He did so in a deceitful way, but he still did so. A Dark king despises weakness, and Drakine's actions made him vulnerable. He harmed me, hid me away, Sinow, Tynan, even Ren, all too weak to protect me. We all fell to the same spell that day, but my husband only sees that

I was taken from him again. Do not remind him of that weakness, or my persuasion will be overlooked."

Xali nodded. The queen looked to the caped man who grabbed Carnick and Xali, stealing them from the queen and depositing them to their room before disappearing.

Carnick grabbed Xali as she swayed, her crown falling to the floor with a crash, then bouncing until it finally stilled. There was something in the way it slowly settled that stirred doubt in him about all that had occurred this day. He dragged his eyes from it and back to Xali. She was staring at it, as if having the same feeling, and Carnick watched her expression. For a moment, she looked defeated, and he didn't like it. She needed to put aside the doubts and find her strength.

"What have I done?"

"Not the first time you've asked that question," he said, pushing a strand of hair back that had fallen free. "You asked a question, Xali. One that should have been held on your tongue but one that you loosed anyway."

"That was a bad move, wasn't it?"

"Apparently."

"Carnick, I don't know what I'm doing. I may have just destroyed it all with one question. How am I to lead a people?"

"Shhh. You made a mistake. That's how we learn. Now, you'll never dare ask the Dark king another question. Although, I must admit I thought you would have learned that lesson with the first uncomfortable question you asked him not long ago."

She laughed. "No, I clearly did not, and I certainly shan't ask another. He's terrifying, Carnick."

"He is, but he would have punished you if he wanted, and he didn't."

She sighed.

"Now, this is our joining eve, the start of our life together. The start of our reign together. Let's put this debacle behind us and do what newly joined people do on their joining eve."

"And what would that be?" she asked with a twinkle in her eye and a raise of her brow.

"We drink heavily and do all those things we were told to save until this eve. Those things that removed your chaste image a bit early."

She giggled, a blush filling her cheeks.

"Do you think you could put the day aside and spend the eve with your new husband, my queen?"

"I think I can do that, my king," she replied, leaning against him and kissing him. It felt good, and as she relaxed into his arms, he prayed this would be one of many eves they would spend in each other's arms and not the beginning of the last.

Four

Ren shifted to the divide between Tenebron and Cirillia, knowing his father would be collecting his thoughts at the ravine. It had been three moons since Xali had been crowned, and in that time, their people had been relocated, and Xali had stepped into her role as queen with the grace and reluctance he had expected. With Carnick by her side, they'd been a reassuring force for their people who were confused and hesitant about what was occurring. They would need time to come to terms with the lies that their history had been built upon, the deceit their royal family had continued to rule under, the atrocities that had not been warranted but had still been inflicted upon the other races.

Homes had been built and towns established all with the help of Ren and the Councils, his mother there beside him, her calm and graceful manner enchanting Xali's people and helping to assuage the doubt and fear that was prone to surface with the changes that were being forced upon them. The people were now settling into their new lives, and Ren knew that Xali would lead them to prosperity.

Knowing he would need to understand their people as he did his own and the Elvin, Ren had taken to spending time with Xali and Carnick. Getting to know them better, he found they were nothing like Drakine had been. In a way, it seemed they were actually growing on him. He'd found Xali's reticence to take the throne endearing, knowing it was what would make her a great queen. It was also a commonality, he having experienced the same hesitation in another life, not ready to accept the weight of his parents' crown. That feeling was stirring in him once again as his ascension neared, an ascension none of them truly knew was coming. Eons had passed since the day he should have ascended. No one knew if the timeline to that day had stopped upon their sleep or if it had merely passed him by.

Slipping silently through the trees, he noted the ravine that had not been seen since before his birth. A ravine that had marked the divide between Tenebron and Cirillia in their history, made whole as his mother had healed it upon her own ascension. Yet here it was, back again like an ugly reminder that their kingdom would forever remain severed, no matter how they tried to mend it.

As he expected, he found his father in the same spot he'd always found him when he was in a pensive mood. It had been that way through his youth and, from what he'd heard, well before his parents had even met.

"Ren," his father greeted him without turning his eyes from the land across the ravine.

"I'm surprised you're not with Mother."

"That would imply you think your mother and I are inseparable."

Ren laughed. "Since when are you not?"

His father shot him a look, and he knew not to push further.

"I merely figured since you'd lost so much time—"

"We'd be making up for it?"

Before the Fates tear you apart again, Ren thought. "Something like that. Where is Mother anyway?"

"Dealing with that mess that caused the loss of time."

Ren looked questioningly at him.

"She's in that monstrosity of a new land and with the annoyance that comes with it."

Ren stifled a chuckle, his father's Dark side always challenged to see past what it judged as indiscretions.

"You mean Xali and Carnick?"

He grumbled, and this time Ren did laugh.

"Father, she's their queen."

"Only because your mother is persuasive."

"I made the final decision."

"As I said, your mother is persuasive."

Ren shook his head, knowing it was futile to argue.

"She won't have an easy reign," his father said. "You know that as well as I."

"Aye, I do."

"There are stirrings in her family. Can you feel it? The undercurrent of deceit."

"Aye, it's there. It's mixed with doubt and distrust. I just can't read from whom."

"Because it's more than one. She'll need to be careful. And her mate will need to stay on guard as will you." He paused then said, "You know what to do if any turn on her."

"Yes, Father." He'd had the reminder countless times. A Dark king's justice was supreme, no matter who the aggressor was, no matter how small the crime.

"There can be no hesitation, your Light side cannot be heeded, the Dark must rise."

"It will."

"Regardless of her mercy or his, our law is final."

"Yes, Father, any threat will be disposed of by me."

"Good, because chaos in that land will only influence ours and sew the seed of doubt in our own people."

Ren stared at the ravine. Before their sleep, when it had been healed, their lands one, the water from the Mother Fate's tears had flowed as a gentle river through the space where it had lain, the land having closed the divide, leaving just enough for the river to move. Now the gentle river rushed far below, the calm of it lost along with the tie of the realms, the land once severed by prophecy, now so by greed and ignorance.

"You're ready, Ren."

"Am I, Father? I once thought I was, but then we slept, and—"

"Now you doubt?"

"I don't know what it is."

"Is it about this new queen or is it something more?"

"A mix of several things."

Ren continued to stare out, feeling his father's eyes on him, hearing his sigh.

"Your mother and I will be fine, Ren."

"Will you? I had thought so before this, but now—"

"We've lived a long life, Ren, even without the sleep. We were blessed to have a second chance to live eons more than we should have. We'll still be together in spirit, we always are."

"That sounds like Mother talking."

He laughed. "She may have had the same pep talk with me."

Ren shook his head.

"She's right. This is your time, and we'll be up there watching you. Although knowing our luck, your uncle will arrange himself right between us, choosing that spot in the endless sky to sink his arse, keeping us apart even in eternity."

"You love, Tynan," Ren said.

"Despise layered with a complex twist of love is more like it. That complicated history lingers."

Ren met his father's eyes, knowing he spoke of the past that had mired his parents' happiness for millennia.

"We'll be all right, Ren. I've come to terms with it, as has your mother. Whatever the Fates have planned for us, we'll accept. Our love is eternal."

Ren relaxed, his father's words removing the last of his doubts. They would be fine, and he would take his place on the throne just as he was meant to, the final piece of his parents' prophecy. His thoughts stirred the revelation he'd had with Paige, that perhaps it wasn't the end or perhaps it was a step in another prophecy, one that involved Xali.

"Father, was there ever talk of another prophecy or one that branched from yours?"

His father turned back to him, his dark eyes heavy with concern.

"Not that I'm aware of. Why?"

"I'm not sure, call it a feeling."

"Instinct?"

"I'm not like Mother. Instinct doesn't guide me as it does her."

His father gave him a slight smile. "You are a mix of both of us, Ren, your logic rules you most of the time, the Dark insisting, but don't ignore your Elvin side. That instinct that rules your mother has proven to be true each time no matter how it confounds the Dark in me."

Ren dropped his gaze and looked out across the ravine.

"What is it you're not saying, Ren?"

"It's just a feeling, like all of this is tied to something greater. They are children of the Fates, the two Fates who created your prophecy, the two who have overseen your every step."

"You forget there were three Fates who created our prophecy. The Mother Fate, her Dark lover, and his brother."

"The same brother whose jealousy would have been a catalyst for banishing any people produced by the woman whom he loved and the brother he scorned."

His father grabbed his arm, turning him to face him. His eyes were rich with ebony and worry.

"You think this is connected."

Ren listened to what his father had called his instinct, that something that nudged him to see past the obvious, to look deeper.

"Yes, I think it is."

"Fates, Ren. The prophecy is supposed to end with you."

"Maybe it does. I may be wrong."

"No, your mother's instinct is never wrong. Ignore it and there are consequences. Maybe it did end with you once, but that ending has been manipulated, changing the course of your path. Tynan's actions before all of this, before your birth, they changed everything. Maybe they fractured the prophecy, made an opening for whatever journey Xali is on."

"One that intersects with my path."

"Exactly."

"What does that mean for you and Mother?"

"Nothing, our path is complete. This is your path…the one you now share with Xali." He ran his hand through his hair. "Fates, that's why you both kept her alive, why your mother insisted."

"Instinct?"

"Instinct. We need to talk to your mother and Daneele; her Keeper would know. He was Keeper of the prophecy until she ascended. If anyone knows, he would."

His father's eyes were frantic, and they held something never seen in a Dark king: fear.

Xali dismounted the horse, giving it a few pats before handing the reins to the stable boy.

"Did you ever think ruling would turn out to be so exhausting," Carnick said, pulling her in for a kiss.

"No, but I also didn't think it would mean what it does for us. I thought I'd be lounging around taking floral-scented baths and relaxing each day while you were off doing your kingly duties."

He laughed. "First of all, there's no way you would ever do any of those things willingly. Second of all, you are now queen, my dear."

"Mmmhmm, this was not what my second-born mind ever imagined."

"I know what it imagined, hours of sword practice and drawing, followed by nights of pleasing your husband." He whispered the last part, nibbling her ear.

"Why do I have to pleasure you? It couldn't be the other way around?"

"Definitely could," he mumbled, kissing her neck.

"Ahhem," her father's voice cut through the desire that was begging for release, sending it crumbling back within her.

Carnick pulled away quickly, and Xali felt her cheeks fill with color. She cursed the reaction. She was a joined woman, one allowed to kiss her husband freely.

"Carnick, I'd like a word with my daughter."

Carnick gave a bow out of habit, something both of them had to retrain themselves not to do. Then he kissed her cheek and walked away, saying, "I could use a nice, scented bath anyway."

He had turned back and winked at her as he said it, and she had to bite her lip to keep from laughing. Her father's intimidating stare left her uncomfortable, and she wished Carnick had stayed by her side. Xali swallowed and drew on her strength, knowing he was testing her, always testing her these days.

She'd offered a home for them, a place of their own, but he and her mother had insisted on staying with them. Carnick's parents doing the same as well as Mendol and Fairenth who had had a quiet joining ceremony after her crowning. It had been three moons. The rest of the family had settled throughout the new land, most not wanting anything to do with Xali. The cousins, who had declared their loyalty to her, now cowering to their parents' command to avoid the plague on their family, the cursed omen who had destroyed their rule. Mendol and Fairenth had traveled to stay with the others a moon ago, an attempt to mend the fracture that now lay between the houses. Their hope had been that the cousins would speak up, allay the elders, and in time, the family would be whole again.

Xali had her doubts, and part of her had wanted them to stay. She wasn't certain why, but she felt a sense of trepidation. Something felt unsettled, and Mendol and Fairenth had ridden directly into that storm. She tried to ignore the feeling, knowing part of it was her father's doing.

Since her crowning, her father had become vigilant, overprotective one might say. Insisting she continue her sword practice deep into the night, practicing her magic until she could no longer keep her eyes open. She would crawl into bed with Carnick, too exhausted to even consider anything but sleep.

Some nights, he would drag both of them out, Carnick's mother joining in the training, but it wasn't helping. Neither of them understood her magic, and Carnick's had changed. While hers seemed grounded in what the immortals called nature magic, his was becoming more like the Dark king's, neither truly knowing what to make of it or what to do with it.

"Have you been out in the towns again?" her father asked.

"Yes, the Light queen was here, helping. She was teaching a village to plant and harvest." Xali looked at her fingers, seeing her nails caked with dirt, as her father took her hand.

"Manual labor is not for a queen. It shouldn't even be for our people."

She snatched her hand away. "It once was. This land was ours at one point, thriving as it is now, providing our food, our water, and now it provides it once again. We don't need nor will we ever again have to rely on the backs of other races for our people to live."

"That woman warps your senses. Fraternizing with the commoners, making you join her, having you work as if you're one of them. It's not right, it diminishes your throne."

"She isn't making me do anything father. Our people are frightened, they have been uprooted, displaced to a land they don't remember—"

"And whose doing is that?" he yelled. "Is that why you're out there? To assuage your guilt?"

She wanted to slap him, her hand jerking slightly to do so; instead, she stood taller, setting her face in a tight, angry scowl.

"I am out there to calm their fears. I will not rule from atop my palace as my people question their place in this world. I will take my place beside them, address their questions, show them who I am, who we are. I will not rule as the others did. My father taught me that the people need a ruler they can trust, one they know puts their needs before their own, one who protects them. I listened, Father, to everything you taught Mendol. Please, trust me. Carnick and I are alone in this. I need to know you see me as they see me."

"Who?"

"The immortals."

He sighed. "I see you, Xaliandri. I always have. I knew you were listening, wanting more, always wanting more than what you were told you were due. You were always a curious child, testing the boundaries, the walls that held our family in place. I knew the day you were born that you were destined for something more. Those full emerald moons that night, casting their light on you, and your eyes," he reached out and touched the corner of her eyes tenderly, "the emerald flecks sparkled in that moonlight before they changed to violet. I knew then that you were special, that the others wouldn't see. They'd already cast you as a bad omen, the ten years you took to arrive, the strange weather that grew in fury until that night. Your mother and I swore to protect you, to keep you from her brother's sight as long as possible, Carnick's mother standing beside me."

Xali couldn't believe what he was saying. All that time and she'd never known.

"When Carnick approached me about teaching you the ways of the sword, I obliged. Your mother argued, saying it wasn't a woman's place to wield a sword, that it would deem you more of an outcast, but I knew it would give you strength. The counter you needed to your dismal powers. It also kept you busy, stopping the questions, shielding you from your uncle's eyes. He, like the others, dismissed you, claiming your union with Carnick would erase the blemish of your birth. You were only a second born after all, what threat could you be?"

He laughed, dropping his hand. "I knew, as did your mother. We turned away from it, ignoring the flowers that bloomed at your touch, the way living things bent toward you, as if you were the sun to their shaded world. Turning a blind eye to the emerald specks that returned to your eyes, claiming the violet. Ignoring what we saw as lesser powers. But they weren't, were they?"

She shook her head.

"Xaliandri, what you've done…" he stopped, wiping his hand over his face. His eyes grew sad, and in that moment, he looked aged, the gray in his beard evident, the creases around his tired eyes there for her to see. Had he always had them or had her recent actions brought them on?

"You've changed everything we were. Stripped us of our position in this world, of the power that is our identity, power that slowly wanes from us as each moon cycle passes. I feel it, the subtle diminishment of it, just as she said would happen. Without our magic, without our crown, what do we have?"

The pressure was building behind her eyes. With all that had happened, she hadn't had time to think on her family's punishment. To contemplate what it would feel like to have the one constant in her life stripped from her, the emptiness it would cause. He was right, she had been the reason for their impending loss. Had she not made the choices she had, they would still be in power. But the immortals would still be asleep, locked in a state that used them to feed the needs of her family. Dying along with the land.

"I won't apologize for what I've done, Father, nor would I undo it if given the chance. It was the right thing to do. If you must place blame, then I will accept it, but Drakine shares in that blame as well. It was his actions, his greed that stripped everything from the immortals and their people, and it was his greed that put us in that position. There is more to our life than magic. Trust me, I lived without it for all those years. You'll all survive, grow accustomed to it, and perhaps find that you serve a different purpose in this life."

Her father's stormy eyes evaluated her. She had the urge to crumble below the weight of their stare, but she stood her ground.

"There are some who won't be content with that answer. Nor are they content with any of the changes you have handed to them. Discontent thrives among us, and I don't foresee it disappearing."

"Is that a threat, Uncle?" Carnick said, coming to stand next to her. She wondered how much of the conversation he'd heard and why he hadn't retreated as her father had directed.

Her father narrowed his eyes. "I would never threaten my daughter, and you would be wise to watch your tongue, Carnick. Your mother and I have aligned with the two of you, but that support can easily be severed."

"I meant no offense, Uncle."

"No, you meant to protect my daughter, something you will need to continue doing. The family is divided over your crowning as well as the events surrounding it. There are fractures beginning to show. It would be wise to remain on guard, to be vigilant."

"They can't hurt me, Father. I'm under the protection of the immortal queen."

"Who does not remain by your side at all times, who from my understanding will be stepping down with her husband when her son takes the throne soon."

"Returning to the Fates," she corrected.

He furrowed his brow, giving her a questioning look.

"It's what immortal rulers do. They depart, return their spirits to the Fates so that the next in line can rule."

"They die? I thought you just proved that they can't die."

"They don't die. I'm not sure I fully understand it, but the Fates remove them from their physical form, their spirits living on for eternity. The stars above are immortals who have returned, others are lingering throughout the land, some merge with the breeze, others with the streams and rivers."

"These immortals have strange myths," her father said, clearly bewildered.

"It's quite sad really. They've been separated for ten thousand years only to return to each other for a few moons before being pulled apart for eternity."

Sadness filled her as she said the words. She had only now come to know the queen but would still miss her dearly. There was something about her that made Xali feel like she'd known her all her life. She had this calm about her that weaved its way into one's heart, settling there.

"Well, then even more reason for you to come practice. If she will not be here to protect you, nor her husband, you are on your own."

"She has me," Carnick said defensively.

"True, but you remain outnumbered and outpowered."

He walked away. Xali knew she was expected to follow, but she couldn't will her legs to move. Was she in danger once again? Her family a threat?

"Come, Xali, we can think on this later," Carnick said. Xali noticed he was glancing around, suddenly aware that she was exposed in the open. "We'll train with your father."

"I thought you were going to bathe and leave me to the training?" she said, wondering why his plans had changed. Did he share her father's concerns?

"I think it would be better to stay by your side."

"You're worried about me as Father is."

"Not until just now."

"Then what steered you from the bath you intended prior to my father's words?" she asked, not believing his words held the full truth.

"Xaliandri!" her father called, noticing they hadn't moved to follow him. "Hasten your stride, we have work to do."

She sighed and looked to Carnick, awaiting his answer still. He took her elbow and began leading her to follow her father.

"That's the reason," he said in a low voice.

"My father?"

"Yes, I had my suspicions about his new infatuation with training you at every chance, and I lingered to hear his words. They confirmed my thoughts."

"So, you were worried about me?"

He didn't answer, and so she stopped, forcing him to face her. Crossing her arms, she waited for his answer.

"Fine. Yes, I'm concerned for the same reasons your father is. We haven't heard from the rest of the family, not even from Mendol and Fairenth, which makes me wonder what they've discovered. Your father is right, the seeds of discontent were sewn the day you woke the immortals, and with your crowning, they have only grown."

"So now what?"

"We do as your father requests and train so that you can defend yourself, and we keep you safe."

"Xaliandri! Carnick!" her father's voice bellowed.

"We'll be right there, Uncle. It is my fault she tarries."

He scowled then walked through an open corridor that led toward the barracks.

"I don't think I can take another day of training," she complained.

"It's necessary until you can master your magic. Plus, I think your father enjoys it. Let him do this, it's his way of helping, and I don't think he knows how else to."

"But we've been gone all day, and I'm exhausted, Carnick. And now you tell me I should be concerned for my safety? All I want is to bathe and wash the day from my skin."

He drew her in and kissed her nose. "I'll keep you safe. No harm will come to you with me by your side. And, as for the bath, once we appease your father, then I will appease you."

She arched her brow.

"I found a stream in the woods, deep enough for bathing and wide enough for two. I promise I will take you there the moment we've finished."

She giggled, feeling her cheeks flush, the stress of the moment fleeing with his words.

"That sounds absolutely wonderful."

"Xaliandri! Carnick!" her father called once again from beyond the corridor, destroying the moment, the weariness returning.

She sighed, knowing that invitation would have to wait and wondering if they'd ever have time to simply be a newly joined couple, the weight of the crown distinct once again.

Ren watched his father pace the room, his mother tensing as Ren told her their suspicions. When Ren finished, they sat in silence, his father's footfalls the only sound. Daneele, his mother's Keeper and Council, stood to the side, tapping his crossed arm as he contemplated the words. As his mother's Keeper, he was the most knowledgeable of the prophecy. Every Light Council had a Keeper, one who was charged with the knowledge of the prophecy, past and future. Ren's Keeper had already been chosen by the Fates upon their awakening, Daneele ensuring he learn the role before he returned himself to the Fates with Ren's parents.

At the thought, Ren grew melancholy, knowing that day grew closer and with it, the day he would be forced to say goodbye to his parents. Paige would be forced to lose her father, Daneele, as he stepped down with them. As though sensing his building emotion, his father's eyes met his. There was a moment of softness before they hardened. Ren looked away to find his uncle's penetrating stare.

A Dark king must shield his emotion, Ren. You would be wise to do so now, his voice echoed through Ren's head.

He called to his Dark power, letting it slide into the crevices his emotion had caused then looked to his mother.

His mother gazed unseeingly at the stone floor, and he wondered where her thoughts had taken her. The footsteps stopped, his father turning to his mother, who brought her eyes up to meet his. Ren saw the fear they held. The prophecy had defined their lives, tested them as no others had been tested. The depth of their love was a result of the hardships they had endeavored through it. Now it threatened their son.

"Daneele," she said, her eyes not leaving his father's, "have you ever seen the entire prophecy?"

"The Fates reveal only what they want seen."

"Do you still have it? The scroll?"

Daneele shook his head sadly. "It was lost when we were overthrown."

A growl escaped his father who Ren knew detested any talk of defeat. "We were not overthrown," he grumbled.

"Do you think Xali's family has it unknowingly?" Ren asked, quick to gloss over his father's irritation.

"No," his mother said, her voice distant. "It is lost. It has not been seen since the ascension. I have no doubt it disintegrated at your birth, our journey concluded."

"Then what is this?" his father asked.

"A branch in the path. Just as Tynan's existence was a branch from the original intent of the prophecy, so Xali's path has been created. Perhaps by Tynan's doing in our lifetime or perhaps she was always there."

"Always in the prophecy?" Daneele asked. "An unseen element as Tynan was?"

"Possibly, or perhaps a continuation of it. Our story was the fruition of the tie between the Mother Fate and the two Dark brother Fates. If this race is indeed a result of the Mother Fate and her lover then all of this is still part of that journey of reconciliation."

"Acceptance of their children among the races the others banished them from," Daneele said.

"Exactly. This is not our prophecy but a path that strayed from it, one that must be walked now that Xaliandri has set the events in motion."

"But we've accepted them, created land for them, even crowned her. What else could there be?" Sinow asked.

"Yes, we have done those things, but this part of the prophecy is Xali's. She must face the tests the Fates give her, just as you and I did. Ren and Carnick are now on that road with her. There can be no turning back, without devastating consequence."

Ren felt the air stick in his chest. He knew the trials his parents had faced, trials that had left them scarred. Now that path was set before him and Xali. He wondered how much of a role he would play in this, if any. His own role seemed uncertain after losing the entire span of what would have been his rule.

He raked his hand through his hair. "We don't even know if I'll ascend. This could still be part of your path."

"No," his mother said firmly as she rose and went to him. "This is your path. Drakine set you off course but perhaps that was all in the Fates' design. Remember, I slept as an infant for thousands of years until your father was born and our lives were both connected to the prophecy. Perhaps you were meant to sleep, to await her time. The Fates have strange ways, but they always serve a purpose."

She brushed his hair back from his forehead, her eyes brimming with her love for him, he only second to his father in her heart, a position he accepted with ease knowing their love was bound by the Fates themselves.

"You will ascend as planned. This is not our path to walk. Time may have continued as we slept, but our place in its flow did not, we are still on that cycle. It will be as it was destined to be."

His heart pounded under the hand she held over it, her words confirming what Ren wanted to delay. It was his time to take the throne and theirs to take their leave. Could he do it? There had once been a time when he had shunned his ascension, refusing to claim that destiny, but the time had finally come. He had the power, the knowledge, the temperament, but he would no longer have them.

Always keen on his emotions, she said in enaigne, their way of speaking silently, *Your father and I will always remain. Our love is too strong not to. We will not be separated.*

You can't know that, Mother.

Call it instinct. Do not worry so on our fate. Reserve your worry for what happens once you take the throne. That is when your true test begins.

Five

The sword glazed over Xali's face as she bent her back to avoid its contact. Bringing herself upright quickly, her blade met Carnick's, the clash of steel ringing through the courtyard. He pushed his weight into the blades, a glint in his eyes. He was enjoying this, and as she took a forced step back, she worried he might just best her this time.

Movement in her periphery threatened to pull her attention, but she ignored it. Carnick was not so disciplined, and his mistake cost him as she quickly countered his pressure, forcing his sword down then disarming him before he could recover.

"Dammit," he complained while she laughed. "I almost had you this time."

"I believe I was the cause of that loss," Ren said, approaching them. "Although I don't think she would have gone down without a fight."

"You've no idea how stubborn she is. She hates to lose," Carnick agreed.

"I can imagine." He studied the two of them. "You don't go easy on each other, do you?"

"We don't play games in training. We train to kill. The Tenebrons are brutal fighters, our army must be able to defend themselves and the—"

He stopped as if realizing what he'd said, having been lost in the past. Xali watched as Ren cocked his brow, the blue of his eyes growing to the color of a night sky.

"Put the swords away. You no longer have use for them. It is time you learned to truly wield the powers you carry. Rulers do not use swords to govern their people. We use our magic."

"My apologies. I didn't mean to—"

Ren raised his hand to stop him. "The past is the past, as my parents taught me, we cannot erase it, we can only learn from it."

"What brings you here today, Ren?" Xali asked, steering the subject quickly from Carnick's words.

"It is time for your true training to begin."

"You're going to teach us?"

"Aye, if you are to rule your people as I rule mine, you must learn to own the blessings the Fates have given you. There are things to come, events on the horizon unseen, and you must be prepared to fight them."

"Events?" Carnick asked as worry filled Xali's chest, her mind going back to Carnick's suspicions about her father's incessant need for her to train. "What kind of events?"

"I do not know, so you need to be ready for wherever this path leads you."

"When do we begin?" she asked.

"We begin now, with shifting. My focus will be with you, Xali, until you've mastered it. Carnick, you will be forced to sit and observe until she's ready. You know your magic, at least the Dark side of it. As so, you can protect yourself."

"And Xali?" Carnick added.

"Not necessarily and I won't take the risk. She will train her shifting ability first and master it. Only then will we move to nature and Dark magic. You both embrace opposite sides of your power, we must have you accept both sides for your true potential to emerge."

And so, they began. It was tedious and Ren was unrelenting, no matter that his insistence wasn't helping. There was nothing controlled about shifting for Xali. She wasn't entirely certain how she'd done it in the first place. Now Ren expected her to understand how the strange ability worked and to use it at will. It seemed like hours of concentrating, of watching him, listening to him, trying to make herself move anywhere. Frustrated, she flopped to the ground and blew a strand of hair from her face.

Carnick, who had been watching the entire time, laughed. "That's something I don't see often. A defeated Xali. I'll have to keep this memory because I won't see it again."

She shot him an annoyed look.

"Tell me, will you give up as an enemy comes at you, sitting in wait for one to kill you?" Ren asked, crossing his arms over his chest. He looked massive from her angle, and she suddenly felt small. He was formidable, towering over her even when she stood. Carnick was taller than she, but the immortals seemed cut from a different mold. Sure, he was strong, muscular, and fit, intimidating in his own right, but Ren and his father, his uncle, they were a presence that filled a room. They were large with chests that seemed twice the size of any of the men in her family, arms that reflected muscles that never seemed to relax, always ready to attack. She looked up at him, his shadow eclipsing her seated frame. As large as he was, she never felt threatened by him, not like she did when she was in his father's presence. There was something comforting about Ren, something she now attributed to his mother, that same calming quality.

She smiled, then replied, "No, I would have cut them down with my sword already."

He couldn't suppress the smirk as Carnick's laugh echoed through the courtyard.

"Get up, your sword will not cut down a Torathar."

"Torathar?"

"Beasts that once roamed these lands, larger than a castle, stronger than even a Darkbearer."

She shuddered, pulling herself to her feet. "And I need to worry about these things?"

He shrugged. "They've been gone for thousands of years, finally turned to ash on a long-lost piece of land that sits to the north of here in the ocean."

"Then I have nothing to fear from them."

"One never knows. Given the right circumstance, they may reappear. They did when my parents were young, after millennia of sleep when they were thought to have been annihilated."

She stared at him, unsure whether she should add these strange monsters to her list of worries.

Laughing, he said, "They are the least of your worries. But no matter the enemy, you must learn to shift. If you are outnumbered, outpowered, shifting will be your last hope. Now concentrate, think of where you want to go and focus on pulling yourself there."

Sighing, she closed her eyes and did as he'd instructed for what seemed the thousandth time. At first, nothing happened, time seemed to drag as she went through multiple unsuccessful attempts, but then as she cleared her mind she thought of her home, the safety of it, the simplicity of her past life, and that strange feeling overcame her. The ground seemed to disappear for a brief instant, the wind taken from her lungs, a wave of nausea drifted through her until she felt the ground below her feet. She wobbled as she opened her eyes, finding herself not outside the home of her youth but standing within a strand of trees.

Ren appeared next to her. "Not bad for your first attempt. Did you mean to come here?"

"Where is here?"

"Southern Tenebron, a place we once referred to as the Banished Realm."

She gave him a confused look.

"Long story," he said. "From that look, I'd surmise this was not where you had intended."

"No, I was thinking of my home, the palace where I was raised."

"Ah," he said thoughtfully. "Well, you are completely out of range but at least you shifted. Let's keep practicing."

"I don't want to go back there, do I?" she asked, having noticed the abrupt way he'd responded to her.

His eyes dropped, then as he brought them back up the blue lightened to an almost iridescent hue before it deepened once again. "No, likely not. Your home is gone, Xali, you know that. We have removed any sign of your family's rule, just as Drakine removed ours when he claimed the kingdom his."

She nodded, having known the truth. It still hurt. Although the recent past held memories that were unpleasant, most of her youth held happy ones.

"We can't go back to the past, Xali. We must both look to what's ahead of us. There is nothing left in the past but ghosts of memories of what once was."

"I know, but that doesn't mean it doesn't hurt sometimes. Things weren't bad, I could have lived that life, taken that role, left things unquestioned."

He studied her, those cerulean eyes seeing deep into her soul. "No, you couldn't have. That's not who you are, even I can see that after only having known you this short time. You weren't meant to follow, Xaliandri, you were meant to lead. The past is gone and with it the innocence it once held, but I have a feeling that innocence was lost long before you decided to wake us."

She laughed. "I will admit I was a bit of a troublemaker."

"I have a suspicion that's quite an understatement."

"Perhaps. Now how do we get back?"

"You shift," he said confidently.

"I shift? We'll be here all night."

"Then so be it."

Grumbling, she tried to concentrate again. This time it came easier, but she still didn't land where she wanted.

"Concentrate, Xali," Ren said.

"I am concentrating," she complained.

After several minutes, she shifted again, only this time she found herself under a tree, its white bark shining bright in the mid-day sun. She took a few steps back, taking in the lush mauve leaves that stood in contrast to the bark.

"I remember seeing this tree the day Carnick and I visited the ruins in Tenebron." She glanced back to see the Dark castle standing where the ruins had been.

"Odd that you would shift here," Ren said, placing his hand gently on the tree as if it were an old friend.

"Why, and why does it look so out of place against your father's castle?"

Ren laughed. "Because it is. This tree was my mother's creation near the end of their journey. It holds an important piece of my history as did its brother, one they called the nightmare tree."

She shuddered at the name.

"Yes, it was not for the faint of heart, especially for those with magic who could feel the trauma it held."

His eyes grew sad for a moment, and as she always did with Ren and his family, she wondered at the sadness, the past that had defined them, leaving a shadow that crept in at times.

Recovering quickly, he said, "Let's try again. This time, focus, the last thing you want to do is accidentally shift in on my father or worse, my uncle. You are mortal after all, and it would be a shame for you to die so soon after all this."

Her mouth dropped at his words, which only elicited a laugh from him.

"They'd kill me?"

"In a heartbeat. Now, shift back to Carnick."

Her mind only on the fear of shifting to her death, she forced herself to try again, praying she didn't open her eyes to find Ren's uncle on the other side. After quite a few more attempts that resulted in her landing in random places throughout the kingdom, she finally found herself high in the mountains of Tenebron. She collapsed, the chill of the air welcoming to her tired body and exhausted mind.

Ren appeared as he did each time. "This is a new one. Do you like heights?"

"Not particularly. How is it you know how to find me?"

"Shifting leaves a trace, a trail of sorts that any of us can follow. Once you are more attuned to the ability, you'll notice it. That and I can sense you. The Dark and Elvin blood within you calls to mine. Once you master your powers, you'll be able to sense me and the Elvin king."

She stared at him, not fully comprehending. He sat next to her.

"Your ancestors were distanced from ours, never afforded the luxuries of understanding other magic and how all of it fits into this world together. Even in the worst of times, the Dark and Light understood that they were necessary to balance the world. Only once has that balance been upset, with the actions of my uncle eons ago. Otherwise, there is a mutual respect. Don't get me wrong, there has also been much discord throughout time, Dark and Light balance but also repel, the two distinctly opposing one another."

"And where do the Elvin fit in?"

"The Elvin are a lesser magic. There have been those in their line whose nature abilities were unique, like my mother and her mother before her, but they are exceptions. The mere fact that the Elvin split their power between multiple heirs, never reunified in their one ruler as ours has always been, leaves them weak. I don't know if that was done purposely or by some construct of the

Fates, but they have no standing against either Light or Dark. They do, however, fit into the balance. The Elvin compliment both sides of magic, they run hot like the fire that stirs my Dark blood and calm like that of my Light blood. They are a piece to the whole that the magic of this world is."

"And me?"

"Well, you are like me, a blending of the powers. Your family, however, tilts to the Dark side because the Elvin will lean that way when Light is not present. You are a blending of the darker halves of this world and that makes you unpredictable, volatile, destructive if the two sides are not balanced within you. The full potential of the Elvin must be released in Carnick to balance the hold the Dark has on him. Just as the Dark must be claimed by you to balance your Elvin."

"But if what you say is true, why would I ever want to do that? Why wouldn't I cling to the calming, good of the Elvin?"

"Because the Elvin are weak on their own. The Mother Fate was one among many Dark and Light Fates. The legends say she was forced to make her children less than they should have been, subservient to the other two magics. That is why she favors my mother, she blessed her with the magic she had wanted to grant to her children. You do not have that luxury, my mother and all now in her line do. You, however, need the Darkness to rule, to wield the power that will protect you. The nature abilities cannot do that alone."

"And if I can't?"

"Then you will die."

Her heart hammered as the last word lingered. He was worried for her life. What was it he knew? What threat was there to her now? She had been named queen, something she'd never wanted. Did that mark her as a target once again?

"Titles can be removed, royalty overthrown, you are in the infancy of a reign that was the result of your family's misfortune. Do not ever think that you are safe."

She rose, her mind replaying his words.

"I don't want this power, I don't want to be queen, Ren."

"All the more reason you'll make a good one."

"But I can't even master this small magic, I can't fathom how the rest will come to me?"

"None of it will until you embrace the Dark side of your power. Trust me, I feared it for a long while, hiding it below the other powers within me. Severing it from them. It wasn't until I owned it, accepted what it was and allowed it to run free, that I reached my full potential."

She stared out at the clouds, the height of the mountain suddenly making her feel small.

"Tell me, Xali, you shifted twice before today, and each time you ended up where you had intended. How did you do it then?"

"I don't know, really. That last time, I think part of it was your mother. Part of it was fear, an overwhelming need to get to her. The first time I shifted, I was scared, everything was overwhelming me, and I just wanted to leave." She thought about it, had she been scared? There had been some fear there but mostly she'd been angry. "No, it was more like anger. I was mad, I wasn't scared that time, I was mad that they wouldn't listen to me, that they wanted to kill me. My own family. And then I was hurt and angry that I'd been betrayed by Carnick, at least I thought it had been him."

"Good." Puzzled by his reaction, she turned to him as he continued. "Take that anger and own it, that's your Dark magic. The part of you who hates weakness, detests injustice, that punishes those who wield it. That's the part of you that will save you. Accept it, call it. Now think of where you initially shifted from today, think of Carnick waiting there for you and find that Darkness."

Before she could respond, he gave her a rough push, sending her from the cliff's edge, falling to her death. In the initial shock, her eyes locked on his before he disappeared leaving her plummeting to her death. She screamed and thrashed her arms and legs as the breath was pushed from her.

Fear swept through her, she was going to die, and he had killed her. She'd trusted him, and he'd turned on her. Had they planned it all along, meant to kill her? Would he return and kill Carnick? This couldn't be happening. She was falling faster, the ground growing nearer.

No, she thought, *he won't kill me. The bastard will pay for daring to hurt me.*

Her fear turned to ire, and something woke in her, a heat that sped through her veins. Anger, a need to punish him, a need to survive. She grabbed it and thought about finding Carnick, finding her way back so she could give Ren a piece of her mind.

Her motion slowed then the base of the mountain disappeared, and she landed to her surprise, hearing Carnick's grumbles as his body took on her impact. They both hit the ground hard.

"Gods, Xali! I think you broke my arm!"

She groaned, pain searing through her. "I think everything's broken," she wheezed, hearing a laugh across from them.

"Graceful," Ren said.

A cooling tingle ran through her, alleviating the pain, her breathing returning.

She scrambled up, yelling, "You pushed me!" Turning to Carnick who was pulling himself up with a befuddled look on his face, she continued, her voice high and frantic, "He pushed me off the side of a mountain!"

Carnick's expression changed to anger. "You what?" he said as he made to attack Ren.

Ren put his hand up, and Carnick's body was stopped by some unseen force.

"It worked, you needed to embrace your Darkness, and you did."

"You did that to test me? What if I had failed?"

"I would have stopped your fall."

"But you were here!"

"He only just arrived when you did."

"But…but—"

"I saw the change, felt the Darkness. I watched from the bottom of the mountain. You were safe the entire time."

She stayed silent, her adrenaline calming.

"You really pushed her from the side of a mountain?"

"She needed to find her Dark magic."

"But I was scared, terrified. How did you know I wouldn't remain that way?"

"Because Dark power detests fear, and it will rise to fight it. Your fear turned to anger, did it not?"

It had, he'd been right. "Yes, just like it did that first time."

"Now that you know how to call it, own it."

"But I don't feel that other part of my magic when that happens, it's like it takes over me."

"Because it does, once you accept it, you then need to let the two merge. Only then will your magic be complete, your full potential met." He smiled. "I think that's enough for one day. I'll be back, and we'll work on that balance. Carnick, I want you to begin to find the Elvin side of your magic, the one your family has buried. Xali can help you. Get some rest, we have much work ahead of us."

"More shifting or something less traumatizing?" she asked. She'd thought he would laugh, but his expression turned serious.

"Until you master shifting, that is all we will train upon."

"But why is that more important than the rest?"

"Shifting is the one thing you share in common with us. Our powers stem from similar sources, but they act differently in you and Carnick. It's as if the eons of blended magic has created something new that we have never seen. The similarities are there, but the final outcome of your power is unique, especially in you, Xali. I don't know that I can teach you what you need to know in order to master your abilities because of this. Shifting I can teach you. Shifting is your lifeline, your line of defense until you've mastered your gifts."

"What is it you fear will happen to her?" Carnick asked, the concern layered in his voice. "Who does she have to fear?"

"Your family still has power, that power has diminished, but it remains until the Fates have drained it. We had thought they'd bind them quickly, but it appears they are not binding them but slowly removing their magic. Until that time, they remain a threat to you in our eyes."

"Our family is no longer a threat. They understand that Xali has been named queen."

"And are they satisfied with that turn of events, all of them?"

Carnick didn't say anything, and Xali wondered if he was thinking the same. Thinking of how most of them had kept their distance, refusing to acknowledge her, the family now broken with her actions, her crowning, the death of her uncle. Thinking on her father's words, his own concerns overshadowing them earlier.

"Exactly," Ren said. "Be vigilant, for you can trust no one at this time."

He was gone on his last word, and Xali let out the breath she was holding, only then realizing that she was shaking. It wasn't over, she'd been naïve to think it so, childish in her belief that it would work out in some happy ending. She'd been wrong. More was coming, death was coming.

Xali was trembling. The quiver of Carnick's own knees threatened to reveal his fear, which Ren's words had invoked. Ignoring it, he wrapped his arms around her and pulled her close, feeling her tension settle.

"Perhaps they're simply paranoid," he whispered as he kissed her hair.

"I don't think immortals get paranoid."

"Overreacting?"

She pulled back and eyed him.

"No?" he said coyly.

"No," she replied, shaking her head, her smile fading. She sighed, the tension returning to her muscles. "What if he's right?" she whispered. "What if they still want me dead?"

He moved his hand to her shoulders. "You are stronger than they are, Xali. They have to come to terms with the change."

"Why? Because they were told to?" She pulled away and began pacing. "Our family has ruled for ten thousand years, whether or not it was legitimate. Now they're being told that's no longer the case, that I, a second born, am to rule our people. They're not going to step aside and give up everything just because they were told to. They will fight, and that's likely what they're planning to do."

"Then they will die, Xali. If they fight against the immortals, they will lose."

"Drakine didn't."

"But no one knows how he did that."

"Uncle Crebant did. I felt it, he was using it on me the night I shifted and went into hiding."

Carnick looked incredulous; this was the first Xali had mentioned such a thing.

"Xali, you're talking nonsense. Whatever spell Drakine used, it died with him thousands of years ago." He took her arm and turned her toward him again, halting her pacing. "Nothing will happen to the immortals again. Even if someone in the family has that spell or even the magic to wield it, the immortals won't succumb to it again. They're too aware of it, too smart."

"Carnick, he didn't say he was worried about them. It's me who is in danger."

Her words hit him squarely, a nudge of fear pawing at him. He shook himself from it.

"They won't let that happen. I won't let that happen."

She nodded, resting her head against his chest.

"I think it's time we talk to our parents, find out what they know. What they've heard."

"Do you think they'll tell us anything? If they even know

anything? They're forced to live with us, but I don't know that your mother's allegiance lies with me. I doubt it ever has."

"My mother is loyal to me, Xali, that makes her loyal to you by default."

"That makes me feel better," she said sarcastically, lifting her head to peek up at him. "Carnick, she does nothing but avoid me. She doesn't want to be here. She only stays for you."

"And what of your father, Xali?"

"My father stays for me. Although I'm tempted to say he'd rather be with his cousins. The way he's been forcing me to train with him day in and day out makes me tempted to send him there."

He started to laugh but then thought about her words. Her father was training her hard, something he'd never done. Sword work had been left to Carnick and Mendol or the guards; no one had bothered to train her powers since they'd decided she wasn't up to their par. That feeling that her father knew something more returned to him. Why else would he suddenly be so obsessed with ensuring she could protect herself? It didn't make sense unless he knew more than he was saying. More than he'd told Xali that day Carnick had stayed back to listen.

"Yes, I think we'd better talk with our parents."

The dining room was silent save for the clink of the silverware. Carnick noticed that Xali had merely pushed her food around. Although their parents were staying in the palace with them, this was the first he'd seen his mother. She'd purposely avoided them, taking her meals in her room, steering clear of their presence. Now, she was avoiding eye contact, stabbing at her food angrily.

Carnick was waiting for Xali to speak, to address them regarding the others in the family, but she remained silent. If she wouldn't speak, he would be forced to do so for her.

His mother slammed her glass down, shattering the stem and the silence that had settled upon them.

"Enough of this charade. I will not be summoned to sup with you as if I am a commoner, especially not by my own son."

She stood to leave, pushing his patience.

"Sit, Mother."

"How dare you!"

He stood and pounded his hand against the table, watching her flinch. "I said sit, Mother."

She glared at him.

"Do as he says, Renia," his father said, standing and blocking her exit.

She swiveled, her face contorted in an angry expression.

"I will not stand for this insolence from any of you."

"You will, and you will sit your ass down in that seat and listen to whatever our son wants to discuss. He brought you here for a reason, and you will respect his wish."

Carnick had never realized how his father towered over his mother until now, having never witnessed him like this. For once, his mother was speechless.

"Sit, woman. None of us are required to heed your commands anymore, so now you will listen to me."

"You are a second born," she hissed.

"No longer," he replied, his eyes stormy.

She looked to Xali's father. "You will stand by and watch me be treated like this?"

"You've been asked to sit, Renia."

"And if Shalinia commanded you like this? Would you be obliged to follow her so quickly?"

Xali's mother stood. "My daughter gets her independent spirit from me, Renia. I am not some slave tied to a tradition that should have died centuries ago and now dies with my daughter's reign."

Carnick's father put a gentle hand on his mother's arm. "Sit down, Renia." His voice was softer, and she turned to him, but not before Carnick witnessed the sadness in her eyes. "It is time for change, change we must embrace, or they will not succeed. We are the past, but Carnick and Xali are our future."

She hesitated then looked back to Carnick. In that moment, she looked broken, as if only now truly understanding the impact of all that had happened. Slowly, she took her seat, the others sitting as well.

"Carnick, Xali, please tell us why you've insisted we be present," his father said.

Carnick looked to Xali, urging her to talk, knowing after what had just happened that she needed to take the lead. She nodded, and he could see the strength in her eyes, her posture changing, bolstered by the actions of his father and her mother.

"The immortals fear I may be in danger, that there is strife within the family that will turn to action against me. We need to know what it is you have heard."

"They are right to be concerned," her father answered. "But you are in no danger."

"What have you heard?" Carnick asked.

"Only rumblings, complaints. They are angry. All they know, all we know is gone, ripped away, leaving us homeless, powerless, and in time, even our magic will fade. It has already begun. They're scared."

"Fairenth and Mendol have been asked to leave," his mother said quietly. "They have been asked to return to your palace. There are those who feel you've betrayed us, both of you. They see Fairenth and Mendol as part of that betrayal."

"But the cousins all said they would stand with me."

"As they were surrounded by the threat of immortals? They murdered one of us, Xali," her father said. "Our cousin, your mother's brother. Did you think that would be forgotten so easily? They are grieving and with your aunt's grief, her ire grows, spreading to the others."

Xali looked to her mother who was looking down at her hands. In all of the madness that had occurred, neither of them had thought on her loss. Carnick wondered at her silence until she raised her eyes to Xali.

"I'm sorry, Mama," she said.

"Crebant was my brother, but…but he was a horrid man. Abusive when we were children and worse into adulthood. I couldn't wait to leave the palace, to marry your father. When he took the throne, it worsened. He lashed out at all of us. Hastrial took his abuse and stood by his side. There was something corrupt in him, something that festered with time. The only reason he hadn't dared move on our province was because he feared the combined power of your father and Renia. He had been whispering in your aunt's ear, swaying her to join him for years. He deserved what he got, they read his guilt right. He would have killed you, Xaliandri, the moment he found you, then he would have turned on us."

Xali's father took her hand. The room was quiet, and Carnick couldn't help but wonder if his uncle's behavior wasn't the influence of his magic. Had he been like Carnick and favored the Dark part of his gifts? Had the power ravaged his sanity? If so, what did that mean for Carnick?

"What do I do?" Xali asked.

"Nothing," her father said, "Renia and I will leave for our cousins in the morn to talk to them on the premise that we are collecting Fairenth and Mendol. We will ascertain the situation then."

"Do you think that wise?" Carnick's father asked.

"They won't dare go against us," he replied.

"As it has been made known to me, the rules no longer apply. They may very well strike against us," his mother said.

"If they dare, they will die," Xali said. All of them turned to her. "The laws of this land are those of the immortals, we are bound to them. Their crimes will be judged by the king and punished accordingly."

"But you are queen, you uphold our laws."

"No, I am queen by their grace, you heard him at my crowning. We yield to their laws."

"Then we'd best pray none of them does anything rash."

The next morn, Carnick and Xali started practice early. She'd been restless the prior night, exhausted but unable to sleep just as he'd been. He'd held her close, feeling the worry in her, unable to relieve it.

As Xali tried once again to help Carnick tap into the nature side of his magic, Ren shifted. They both jumped, neither having grown accustomed to the sudden appearance of the prince.

"Good morn, Xali, Carnick."

"Do you ever simply use a gate entrance?"

"No need, I knew where you were."

"What if we'd been indecent or occupied?" he asked.

Ren shrugged. "Nothing I haven't unwittingly seen from my parents or uncle for that matter, although you two seem more predisposed to contain that sort of thing to your quarters, unlike them."

Carnick watched Xali's cheeks fill with color and tried not to laugh at her sudden modesty.

"Now, I didn't come here to embarrass your wife, although it is refreshing. We will train today. Xali, you will continue to work on your shifts, Carnick, we will hone your magic."

"I won't be spending the day with your mother again? Only training now?"

He could hear the disappointment in Xali's voice. She'd grown attached to the queen since she'd awakened, an attachment he attributed to that strange connection they'd had when the immortals had been asleep.

Ren's expression grew sad for a moment before he covered it. "No, as my ascension is less than two moon cycles away, if our timeline is still in place even after the long sleep, then their time here is limited. They have decided to spend their remaining days with each other."

"They die when you ascend?" Carnick asked, still not truly understanding the process.

"Not truly, they will return their bodies and souls to the Fates, as it is required upon each ascension. No two kings can live at one time."

"That's so sad," Xali said.

"They've lived long lives together, the Fates blessing them."

Carnick couldn't imagine being forced to give up his life, to give Xali up, to never hold her again. He suddenly felt a deep sadness for the king and queen.

They heard movement behind them, Ren's eyes already drawn away from them before Carnick's ears registered the sound.

"Your highness," Xali's father said with a courteous nod.

Ren said nothing but gave a brief nod back. Carnick could feel the change in Ren's power. It was clear he and Xali were on good graces with the prince but not the rest of their family. The betrayal of Drakine ran deep.

"Renia and I are traveling west to talk with our cousins. Since they chose to settle furthest to the coast, it will take us several days to travel. We will then stay as long as necessary to allay their concerns and root out any betrayal before returning with Mendol and Fairenth."

"My mother is going willingly?" Carnick asked.

"She has agreed to it for your sake. Your mother may be slow to accept these changes, but she still loves you, nephew. She will do what's needed to ensure you stay safe."

He left without another word.

"He's a man of many words, isn't he?" Ren joked. "Much like my father. The Darkness rules your family now, the Elvin succumbing to its relentless pressure."

"Does the Darkness corrupt?" Carnick asked, thinking on his uncle Crebant and what Xali's mother had told them the prior night.

"In some yes. We now suspect Drakine was under its influence. We sensed the two powers, but the mix in the blood of your kind made it hard to judge him. Just as it makes it hard to discern which way either of you will lean."

"What happens when one becomes corrupted?"

"The Darkness overtakes them, madness abounds. Your uncle was on the cusp of it. In mortals, it will eventually destroy them."

"And in immortals?"

"The most terrifying Dark kings are the mad ones. My uncle was one of them for a long time, the Darkness ruling him. He nearly killed my father, and he did kill my mother once, she only returning by the grace of the Fates. He brought our kingdom to its knees, destroyed it all. If not by the will of my parents and their devotion to each other, there would have been nothing for Drakine to overthrow."

A faraway look crossed his face then he added, "But that was all in the past, a past the Fates have changed, a past that never involved your people. Would it have? I wonder…or is this part of it all…"

His words stopped, but his eyes stayed distant, as though he were talking to someone else, someone beyond their sight. He stayed quiet, and Carnick looked to Xali who shrugged, just as bewildered as he was. Eventually, his eyes refocused on Xali. He studied her. As Carnick watched, it dawned on him that although this man looked to be his age, he was far from it. The ancient wisdom his piercing blue eyes held led him to believe they held a vast number of years, thousands beyond Carnick's comprehension.

"Your path is tied to mine, Xaliandri. We believe it is no coincidence that Drakine came to our shores, no coincidence that we slept until you were ready to be called. The Fates don't work in coincidences."

"Who is we?" Carnick asked.

"My parents and I. Their prophecy is ended, but I was always the end of their path. My path is just beginning, and you are part of it, I'm certain of it, we just don't know where you fit in."

"That's who you were talking to?"

"Yes, my mother."

"You can talk to her in your mind all the way from here?"

"Yes, enaigne has no boundaries."

Carnick set aside his wonder at this new information and asked, "What do you mean, she's on your path?"

"It has always been suspected by my parents that the Fates have their own prophecy for me. A destiny that goes beyond the joining of the three powers. Nothing has ever been found, but the Mother Fate made mention of it once to my mother, and so we've waited for them to show us my path."

"Prophecy?" Xaliandri said. "That can't be a good thing. Why me?"

"No, it may not be. My parents faced an arduous path, one they would not wish on anyone."

"Gods," Carnick said.

"Fates," Ren corrected. "I don't know why you were chosen, but you have been, and now we traverse this journey together, no matter the cost."

"The consequences will be disastrous if it's not followed," Xali said. "That's what your mother said when she spoke to me."

"And she knows better than anyone."

"So where does this leave us?" Carnick asked, his concern for Xali now two-fold.

"Nowhere different than where we stand. We train you both and follow the path that we're already on."

"Follow a path about which we know nothing, one that began ages ago and doesn't seem to have an ending," he muttered.

"So, it is with the Fates. They are not always clear, never easy on us, and the journeys they set us upon are often long."

"How long did it take your parents to reach the end of theirs?" Xali asked.

"Too long."

There was nothing left to say, Carnick not wanting to know how long too long was. Ren's parents were immortal, and he and Xali mortal. Whatever this was, he didn't think the end would linger. Whatever was coming, was coming soon, and neither he nor Xali was prepared for it.

They trained straight through the morning, Xali honing her shifting and Ren working with Carnick to draw the Elvin power to which he kept alluding. Carnick struggled to find a connection to it. Try as he might, there was nothing separate that he could draw upon. Nothing more than that miniscule amount he'd been able to find when Xali had transformed the shrine, and even that wasn't coming to him this day. He couldn't do any of the things Xali could do. Any time he came close to the flowers with his magic, ones she'd raised so easily, they would wither and die. He'd been trained since early on to ignore anything that resembled a lesser power. It had been drilled into him that the power he held now was the only power, that one did not seek or identify lesser powers. It was death to do so. If it had ever been there, it was lost to him.

Finally, frustration and exhaustion reached its peak, and he raised the ground in his fury, tearing it asunder. Ren moved next to him and studied the new terrain, running his hands along the exterior.

"It's not coming to me, Ren. No matter how many times I focus, it's not there."

Xali shifted, landing on top of the newly formed hill and losing her balance at the unexpected slope of her landing spot. She rolled down, lacking her usual grace, and Carnick caught her.

"Next time, shift out of your fall and land on your feet," Ren commanded, still examining Carnick's creation. "Perhaps I'm looking at this the wrong way. Get some rest, I'll be back once I've thought this through clearer."

Then he was gone, leaving them both befuddled.

"What was that about?" Xali asked.

"I honestly don't know."

She glanced at the results of his frustration then with the graceful sweep of her hand, it settled in a soft movement, cresting then flowing back to reform, giving the impression that Carnick had never transformed it.

Turning her eyes back to him, the emerald specks sparkling, she smiled, and his heart swelled.

"I can't do it, Xali. No matter how hard I try, there's nothing similar to what either of you describe. I don't have those abilities."

She reached up and kissed him. "Let's call it a day. We're both tired, and I could use a long soak in a hot bath about now."

He pulled her to him. "A hot bath sounds wonderful," he said, kissing her neck. "Would you like some company?"

She raised her brow, her smile spreading. "That's a possibility," she said seductively.

All thoughts of prophecy and magic fled to be dealt with another day.

Six

Ren was restless; he'd spent the remainder of the day pondering Carnick's magic and Xali's, his mind trying to make sense of why both were so different from what he'd seen and felt from their family. Each leaned toward Dark or Elvin, not the mix. Was his mother right, had his family never realized their full potential or had something been lost long before they'd arrived on these shores? But why the disparity between the two? He was missing something.

"Come to bed," Paige said, drawing her arms around his waist and leaning her head on his back. He rested his hand on hers. "You're fretting again."

"Aye, sleep will not be mine tonight."

"Is this what I have to look forward to when you ascend? Sleeping alone each night?"

He laughed then turned to face her so that she was now in his arms. Kissing her, he relaxed. She had a calm about her that settled his powers, the warring that still occurred for dominance within him. It was no longer all-consuming as it had been in his younger years, but it was still there, the dichotomy between Dark and Light, a constant storm.

Her cerulean eyes searched his. Pushing her hair back, his fingers delaying in its softness, he said, "I can promise you I won't leave you to sleep alone."

"Good because you'd have my wrath to reckon with if you did."

"The wrath of a Cirillian is not a very powerful threat, my dear. Now if you were Tenebron, then I might be concerned."

She hit him playfully before he pulled her to him, stealing another kiss. It was short lived, the weight of his thoughts still present, and he dropped his forehead to hers.

"Get some sleep, Paige."

She lifted his chin, her eyes laced with worry, but she said nothing, knowing well enough that he could not be swayed from his state. She kissed him once more then left him, her hand skimming his as she turned.

He dropped into a seat and ran his hand through his hair. What was he missing? He needed to speak to his parents, but they'd left the kingdom in his hands, taking their little remaining time to be with each other. He couldn't disturb them.

He wondered if there was someone else as keen to this as his parents then thought he might just know who. He stood and shifted to the Dark keep, the Darkness that it held calling to his Dark power, the mere presence in Tenebron feeding it. He let the sensation roll through him, then looked around. He'd landed in his father's office, where many of the discussions that had shaped his past had taken place. As a child, he'd watched his father, the authority and power he held always overwhelming him. His father was a terrifying presence who commanded obedience. Ren had struggled for a long time with that part of himself that he'd inherited from his father. He was more like his mother than he'd wanted to admit, more than his father liked. He had feared the Darkness and what it would do to his other powers, to him.

He ran his hand along the great desk, wondering if he would ever sit here as his father had. Would he be the same man, inspire the fear needed to rule Tenebron? Would that Darkness remain balanced with the Light and Elvin needed to rule the other two realms? The legacy he'd been charged with, to rule all three kingdoms, was daunting. With his parents, there had been two rulers, two to split the work, the control, the sheer breadth of land in the kingdom. Now the Fates had left it in his hands. He couldn't even figure out this Xali conundrum—how did they think he'd fare with running a kingdom as vast as theirs?

"I can sense your doubt all the way to my quarters, Drostiren," his uncle said, interrupting his thoughts. "What brings you to the Dark keep this late and burdened with unrest?"

"I'm not having doubts, Uncle."

"Could have fooled me. The air in here is thick with it."

"I shouldn't have come here."

"Yet you did. Why?"

Ren sighed as his uncle sat, his black eyes awaiting his answer.

"To find you. I didn't want to disturb Mother and Father."

"So, you pull me from the arms of my mate. That's thoughtful."

"Sorry," he said before his uncle slammed his hand down on the chair arm, shattering it.

"Dark kings don't apologize! You are too close to ascension to forget that. One cannot rule Tenebron with apologies."

Ren felt the rush of Darkness fill him in response to his uncle's anger.

"That's better. Tenebron is not the place for Light power, even if it is dwindled in numbers at the moment. When the population returns to what it once was, you will need the Darkness. You are a Dark king, and you must never forget that."

But I'm not a Dark king. I'm something else, he wanted to argue, but he remained silent, knowing his uncle only recognized the Darkness, unlike his parents who understood the blend of powers he held better than anyone.

"I don't think you came here to have me remind you of that, however. What's on your mind, Ren?"

He sat in his father's chair, feeling the worn comfort of it, missing him for a brief moment, even though he wasn't gone yet.

"I'm perplexed," he said, letting the sensation slip away.

"Go on."

"The power Xaliandri holds is distinctly Elvin, there are glimpses of Dark power but nothing that blends with the Elvin. Only moments when it takes the lead, like when she shifts. That power is drawn from her Dark power. The Elvin can't shift, only Dark and Light."

"And we know they're not Light."

"Correct," he said, rising then pacing as he talked through it. "Then there's Carnick. I can sense the Elvin, but the Darkness overshadows it. He can move the land, can destroy stone, shape it into something completely different. All of that is nature-based but with Dark overtones, giving him abilities that the Elvin and even Xaliandri do not have."

"His magic is the same as his family's, is it not?"

"Yes, but he raised Father and you—"

"Perhaps he is more attuned to the Darkness than his family. Drakine's power was a combination of both Elvin and Dark. We discerned that early on. If what Violissa says is true, then those powers came from the Mother Fate and the Dark Fate. If that's the case, then Carnick's power is just as all of his ancestors, a warped blend of the two powers, and nothing more."

"Then how do you explain his ability to awaken us?"

His uncle was pensive, and as Ren awaited his response, he was glad he'd chosen to come here for answers. His uncle was a thinker, a problem solver, he enjoyed the challenge. He hunched forward in his chair, clasping his hands.

"Before your birth, when Chastity was sent here by the Fates, there was a boy who inadvertently ended up with a mix of powers warped like the ones we see in Carnick and his family. He could do things we'd never seen, things not within your mother's abilities to do with the land. It was very similar to what we've seen Carnick and his family do, that violation of the land as your mother calls it. I'd forgotten as had they. That wrenching of the land is the Dark magic. They all lean toward it, Drakine did. Your father and I felt it, that's why we were concerned."

"So, if they lean toward the Dark naturally—"

"Then your mother is wrong, a very unlikely thing for her…or something's changed within them over time. The Darkness took control, using the nature abilities and bending them."

"Then how do you explain, Xali?"

"Xali is what they originally were, a subtle blend of the Dark with the Elvin, the beauty of the Elvin tie to nature, seducing the Dark to stay in the undercurrent. She is the origin of their kind. What they were meant to be."

Ren stared at his uncle, the revelation stunning him. It left too many unanswered questions, however.

"So, if the others lean to the Dark, any of them could have awakened us."

"I don't think so. It was meant to be Carnick, the two of them. He's tied to her somehow but not in the way you've been looking. He will never know the nature side of her gifts as she does. That's why he struggles so. Whatever caused their ancestors to turn to the Dark, to seal away the Elvin, it is done, and there is no changing that. Their future lies in Xali's hands, in her heirs. That's why she needed to be crowned queen, why your mother's instinct guided her to do so."

"Prophecy…all of it tied to prophecy."

"The Fates have their ways, Ren. We are forced to play our roles until whatever outcome they deem is completed. Trust me, it's a hard road. Shame I won't be here to see it to fruition," he said, rising.

That surprised Ren. "Wait, I thought you were staying. I thought…" *at least you would still be here*, he wanted to say but refrained.

His uncle smiled. "My place is with your parents, the three of us tied with that damned prophecy. No matter how selfish I want to be with thoughts of staying on with Chastity, I won't. I swore my allegiance to them upon my redemption and there it remains. I will return myself to the Fates as they do."

"And Chastity?"

"Will do the same. She's lived far longer than she'd ever imagined. She's ready to transition with me."

"But you'll lose each other, just like my parents will."

His eyes filled with sadness for a brief flash, the lush brown softening before the ebony filled it.

"Chastity will hunt me down, Ren, you know how persistent she is. You don't come to love the most hated Dark prince in our history without tenacity. She'll find me, and when you see two blazing stars merge up there, you'll know we're having fun."

Ren shook his head and laughed. "I'll be sure to look the other way."

"Good, although it could be quite a show. Get some rest and get back to your wife. I'm going to get my fill of my mate before I'm stuck in some other form in which I can't enjoy her touch."

He shifted, leaving Ren to his thoughts. He had more direction now and what his uncle had said made sense. He was, however, left with many more questions than even the best night's sleep could answer.

Xali stared at the water, her reflection looking back intently, although her eyes didn't register it, for her mind was elsewhere. It had been three days since their last training with Ren, and she was restless. Carnick had left to handle an issue in the nearest town, insisting that she stay, which had irritated her, but she'd acquiesced.

She wasn't doing anything productive here; in fact, she was feeling a peculiar sense of drowning under the weight of everything that had happened as her mind finally was given the quiet to comprehend it all.

Sighing, she rose from the side of the pond. She didn't want to be here, a prisoner in her own palace and in her own mind. Looking down at her hands, she wondered if she should practice her magic. Ren had said shifting was her best defense until she mastered the rest, but was it safe to practice without him? Would she end up stuck at the top of a mountain again with no way down, freezing to death while Carnick searched desperately for her?

She shook the thought from her head. "Don't be ridiculous, Xali," she chastised herself.

Closing her eyes, she thought of where she wanted to go but nothing came to mind. The gardens where she'd been crowned flashed in her head, although that was the last place she wanted to be. She felt the sensation of movement and then the ground below her feet.

"What the Fates!" She heard as pain seared through her body, bringing her to her knees. An inferno raged through each of her cells until the pain receded replaced by the gentle cool touch of healing magic.

Opening her eyes, she found herself in the gardens, the splash of the fountain filling her ears. She looked up to meet the king's eyes.

What have you done, Xali? she thought as his black eyes glared at her.

"Xali," the queen said, rising from the stairs where she'd been seated, ones that led to the fountain, and placing a hand on her husband's arm.

"You risk death with a move like this, Xaliandri," the king said.

She rose from her knees, hoping their residual shaking wasn't noticeable. His words brought back Ren's warning about shifting anywhere unwittingly near his father or his uncle. Would she have been dead if it were the uncle whom she'd disturbed?

"I...I...I'm sorry. I shouldn't have tried that without Ren to direct me. I don't know how I ended up here, it just popped into my mind, and then, well, here I am."

The queen smiled at Xali, but the king's expression didn't change. He crossed his arms, and Xali realized what a massive presence he was; he seemed to engulf the entire room.

"And here you are," he said in a grumble.

It was only then that Xali remembered Ren saying that his parents were taking their final days together alone. She'd disturbed them during their time. Fates, she was so stupid for thinking she could shift alone.

They looked at each other as Xali felt her embarrassment rise.

"I'll be going now, I'm so sorry." She tried to shift but felt nothing, the two of them continuing to look at each other.

They're talking to each other, she thought as the king's aura lightened. The queen smiled, and he gave her a kiss before he disappeared.

"He didn't have to leave. I'm trying to go. I just...I don't..." She was flustered, but she didn't know why she was such a mess.

"Shhh, you're fine, Xaliandri," the queen said, coming toward her. It seemed so strange how she seemed to float on the ground, gliding when she walked, her steps so graceful. As she approached, Xali felt the calm that always settled over her when she was in the presence of the queen.

"If you're here, there's a reason you're here."

"But you and the king, this is your time together, and I interrupted that."

"Nonsense. Sinow and I have had more time than we could have imagined together. A few moments apart will not harm us." She took Xali's hands. "Now, what brings you here and why do you appear so restless?"

"Impatient might be the better word for it," she answered honestly.

"Hmmm, what is it you seek, Xali?"

There was something about the queen that gave her a sense of comfort, that she was safe to say what she wanted, to express how she was feeling. It was a strange thing, something to which she wasn't accustomed.

"My place," she answered honestly.

The queen smiled, her eyes sparkling. She released Xali's hands and reached up to let her fingers touch Xali's hair, guiding a silver strand out so that they could both see it.

"You already know your place, you always have, you are a daughter of the Mother Fate, marked by her silver locks and the emerald specks in your eyes, just as my eyes mark me."

"But what does that mean? What does any of this mean? Ren is talking about prophecy, and I can't even find my place in this world, my purpose."

"Ah, but your purpose has yet to be fully shown to you, to any of us. It took me many years to realize where I fit into the grand design, what my true purpose was. At first, I only saw the surface, the bonding of my heart to Sinow's, a forced arrangement you might say, by the Fates. I couldn't see the gift they were giving me, the love of a man who is the very air I breathe, the other half of my soul. I only saw the demands of prophecy, the restraints on my free will. Look beyond the surface, give yourself over to where you are, to the purpose they have in store for you. Fighting it will only delay it, trust me."

"When did you finally know?"

"It's hard to recognize it when you are part of it. It wasn't until the very end that I knew, that we both knew. You are in the midst of it, your first steps taken when you were brave enough to wake us. Your place is here, your purpose still in motion."

Xali sighed, the answer not relieving her frustration.

"I don't think it was chance you shifted here. Now, you will spend the day with me."

"No, I can't. I need to get back. Carnick will worry, and you, you need your time with your husband."

A faraway look crossed the queen's face for a moment then her eyes refocused on Xali. "It is done, Ren will alert Carnick of your whereabouts. There is something he needs to discuss with him anyway, and this offers that chance."

Xali wanted to ask, but the queen stopped her.

"He'll discuss it with you when you return. Come, walk with me."

Xali followed her out of the open garden, on into the field of wildflowers that spread across the grounds. It was a complete change from the ruins that had once been here. They walked in silence through the field then onto a path that sloped down. As they treaded the path, she could see a valley shimmering in the sun, the river she'd freed gently coursing through it. She turned and saw the glorious Elvin castle tucked in the side of the cliff. Just as it had in her dream before she'd saved the queen, it gleamed gold and white, nature climbing its way throughout the balconies, flowers on vines that hung from banisters, tree limbs that swept through open windows, their bark layered with blooms. It was breathtaking. To the side of it, the waterfall crashed down in a comforting splash that settled gently upon the land below, flowing to meet the river that snaked along the valley floor.

She looked beyond it, past the cliffside and the trees that went on for miles in every direction, no longer contained, no longer hidden from the rest of the world.

"The guardian wall is gone. I'd forgotten you destroyed it when you woke. All that was contained behind it has now sprung to life."

"It took thousands of years for us to unite the realms, now they are back as they were during our reign, as they should be."

She turned back to the valley. "And this?"

"Is the Elvin Enclave. As it once was before Drakine left it in ruins. Their numbers are small now, but in time, they will fill the valley as they once did."

"Why are you showing me this?"

"As proof that you have a purpose, that it has already begun.

These are your brothers and sisters, Xali, the same blood runs through them as in you and as in me. The blood of the Mother Fate, the Elvin. You freed them, restored them to their rightful place in this world, took them from hiding so they were free to live once more. Do not question your purpose. It is powerful."

The queen's eyes were shining an emerald that was nearly blinding.

"Let us visit, I believe you have some nature gifts that may need discovering still."

The queen began walking down the slope toward the village, but Xali stood frozen, taking it all in. This was the world the great king had destroyed. He had taken the beauty from it, the people, the castles, the immortals, and in its place he had erected a wall and severed a kingdom that had once spanned the breadth of this entire land. Xali hated him for it. He was like a stain she couldn't wash from her skin, a badge of shame she was forced to carry. One she would cut away and eradicate, just as he had done to the realms of this world.

Xali spent the day with the queen in the Elvin Enclave, Narilen, king of the Elvin, joining them. It was good to see him and to see the others out of hiding and in their natural environment. He'd given her a hug when he'd first seen her, calling her Slamiara, the Elvin word for savior. As she'd gone through the day, she'd noticed the Elvin all bowed their heads slightly in her presence. It made her feel uncomfortable; people had always bowed in the presence of her family, but it had never been something she'd embraced.

She learned much of the Elvin connection to nature, more than Narilen had been able to teach her, the queen's magic greatly enhanced from his. Drakine had ensured the ruling line of the Elvin was left weakened the day he had attacked them, attempting to kill the royal family and annihilate their kind. The infant princess left behind had no one to help coax her true powers to fruition, and so it had remained with every child born to the line from that point.

The queen taught her and Narilen beside her, both of them learning what had been hidden from them. Xali found it odd that she held two powers, yet her nature magic came so easily. She could feel the Dark now that she'd recognized it with Ren, but it was like a soft undercurrent to her magic that simply was present, the nature side of her dominant. The queen seemed to notice this and, as if she held the same Dark undercurrent, she taught Xali how to let it feed her nature gifts. With her help, she moved beyond the simple control of the world around her to a more complex one, overshadowing even Narilen with her abilities. Carnick had been right, even the weather seemed to heed her call, and as a rainbow crested through the valley, the queen gave her a warm smile.

"If only you had been born a few thousand years earlier," she said. "We could have had more time to explore how truly connected you are to the Mother Fate's magic. She blessed you as she blessed me, with her own gifts. You are powerful, Xaliandri. It will continue to come to you as you grow more comfortable with it, and once it does…well, you will make a formidable queen."

Xali didn't know what to say. It was true what she'd tapped into this day was greater than she'd expected, but she still felt small, weak compared to the queen, even to Narilen.

The queen took her hand. "Continue to practice, listen to the land, the way it calls you, the gentle words of the wind as it beckons for your attention. The world is your magic, and once you accept that, it will gift you with everything you were meant to be. Do not ever think yourself weak to anyone in our world, for once you do, you weaken yourself, and they will see it."

She turned away and began working with Narilen again, the two calling a sapling from the bare ground and coaxing it to flourish to a tree that grew to tower high above them. Xali stood aside, lost in thought as she contemplated the queen's words. Was she stronger than the Elvin king? Was she meant to be as powerful as the immortals? The queen had said she shouldn't think herself weaker than anyone in their world. Did that include the immortals? It didn't seem possible; they were awe-striking with their abilities, and she could merely cause a rainstorm or urge the land to move.

She watched as Narilen worked on the tree, only then noticing that the queen was teaching the two of them differently. Narilen focusing on the land, the plants that graced it, the river that flowed through it, the physical pieces of it. With Xali, it was the sky, the wind, the weather. Perhaps, there was truth to her words, perhaps Xali's powers were different from the Elvin yet still connected to them.

As the day grew long, the sun lowering in the west, they said their goodbyes, the queen walking her back to the garden where she'd shifted earlier. Xali took the quiet moment to ask a question that had been on her mind since they'd entered the enclave.

"Why do they bow toward me? My people are the reason they were forced to hide."

"Ah, but you freed them, and you awakened me, their high queen."

"High queen?" She'd remembered hearing the term before but not its meaning.

"Aye, Narilen is king, a very distant cousin of mine, but I am the true queen of the Elvin, the overseer of their care and prosperity. My connection to the prophecy and the Mother Fate deems it so. As too, Ren will take my place as high king. It will remain so with each future heir in our line."

"Then why is Narilen, king?"

"My mother had a twin brother who was born first. As in your house, birth order matters to the Elvin, and he was made king when their father died. My mother would have remained princess but for her marriage to my father, king of Cirillia. As I am half Elvin and the Light child in the Fates' prophecy, it is I who first freed them from a cursed sleep when Sinow and I joined. Thus, they fall under my rule, regardless of who their born king or queen is. The Fates have declared Sinow and I rulers of all realms in our world."

"Mine, too?"

"Yes," she answered without hesitation.

They had reached the gardens and now stood before the fountain.

"Your people only live because I willed it so," the king said, stepping into the space.

Xali jumped slightly, not having seen him there, then wondered how he'd heard the conversation. Had he been there, listening the entire time they'd talked?

"Then why name me queen? Why have an Elvin king?"

"Each realm must have its own rule, each race different, the only exception to that will be Ren who is half Tenebron, half Cirillian."

"And a bit Elvin," the queen added.

"Aye and Elvin. He will rule the two realms as you will rule yours and Narilen his. Ren's command, however, just as mine and Violissa's are now, shall be the final judgment. Your people need someone like them, one of their own who knows your history and your ways. That knowledge is vital to the flourishing of your realm. Without it, who they are as a people ceases to exist, their ways eliminated."

"As we did to your people?"

His eyes grew blacker. "Yes, but our people are resilient and, thankfully, a few held onto the memories of their past."

"So, I am a figure head?"

"You are a leader. You will face the hard decisions that come with ruling. Your land, your people, your laws autonomous. If, however, our laws are impacted by yours, our people threatened, our land threatened, the very laws we rule by ignored, we will step in. We will punish as needed, kill as needed. Crime is not tolerated in my world."

A chill shivered through her, a part of her called by his words. She had no doubt he was serious.

"I warned you when you accepted the throne that we would

supersede you if need be."

She swallowed nervously, trying not to show her fear, wondering once again what she'd gotten herself and her people into. This man was terrifying, the direct opposite of his wife with her warm, calming demeanor.

"Shhh, Sinow, you're worrying her."

"She should be worried, and she should know to fear me and Ren."

"Fear is a good word for it, but it's mixed with a bit of exhilaration," she said bravely.

"That would be the Dark blood in you. Keep it in check, or I'll be forced to deal with it my way."

He shifted, and Xali looked at the queen for explanation.

She only smiled a knowing smile. "It is time for you to head home now. Time for me to calm my husband's mood."

"Is he always like that?"

"Intense?"

Xali nodded.

"It comes with the territory. Dark kings don't take things lightly, they are serious, and their sentences swift and deliberate. Ren will be the same. Don't confuse his Light side with the Dark he keeps silent. He is a mix of me and my husband. He may favor the Light side, but the Dark is always waiting, watching, and ready to strike."

Seven

Carnick drew the horse to a halt and looked upon what had once been the shrine of the gods. He had left earlier in the day to resolve a land dispute in one of the newly settled towns, but riding back to the palace, he had felt the need to return to this place. He had not done so since the day Xali had transformed it, the day he had helped her erase the structure that had been a place of worship for him since as far back as he could remember. It was gone now, replaced with a garden of sorts, one that stood as a gateway to their land.

He dismounted and walked toward it, glancing back at the cliff-side that stood as the divide between their land and Tenebron. It was a distinct separation, the land above shadowing theirs. A path had been made leading up the steep incline, flowing along the cliff until it reached the upper boundary of Tenebron. Not that any in their land would venture there again, the threat of the Dark king's wrath too much of a deterrent.

He turned back to the shrine where it blended in the field of lush grass and flowers that the queen had created. It was beautiful, welcoming, a comfort as their people had settled to the land of their ancestors. Still, there was something that bothered him about it, as if it weren't meant to be there any longer. That it should still be replaced with the shrine, with the symbol of the gods he and his family had prayed to since the beginning of their history. He knew the Fates existed, that his people had been created by them, yet the thought of them settled oddly in him, different than the gods had. Xali had embraced them fully, why couldn't he?

The air around him changed, turning hot so that his skin warmed as it would before the holy lands had been transformed. There was something in that warmth, something familiar that called to a part of him. His eyes drifted to the mountains far in the distance, standing too far to see distinctively. He couldn't pull his eyes from them, waiting for something he couldn't define, something unseen.

The air cooled, and the clouds that had formed above him broke, the mid-day sun returning. Shaking the feeling away, he returned to his horse, the need to be with Xali strong. He gave one last glance at the former shrine, noting how the shadow of Tenebron overtook it, muting the beauty, then he headed home.

When he returned, Ren was waiting for him in the courtyard. His mind went immediately to Xali.

"Ren, is something wrong? Is Xali all right?"

"Yes, she's fine. I was told to let you know she's with my parents, spending the day with my mother." Carnick's confusion must have shown, for Ren continued, "It seems she attempted to shift on her own and ended up surprising them. She's lucky my mother was there, or I can't say she'd have fared so well."

"Gods," Carnick said, running his hand through his hair.

"Fates," Ren corrected, raising a brow.

He studied Carnick for a moment. The silence was unsettling, and Carnick wondered briefly if Ren could see the thoughts he'd had at the old shrine, the doubts that still lingered. If he did, he made no mention of it.

"So, you've come to deliver a message. Should I also expect to spend the next few hours training? If so, a good mug of ale might be in order first."

"The duties of a king often require the respite of ale, or so I've observed," Ren said with a grin as two metal mugs brimming with the froth of ale on the top appeared in his hands.

Carnick couldn't keep his mouth from dropping. "You can make ale? Out of nothing? How did anyone ever think immortals were lesser with an ability like this?" he asked, taking a mug.

He couldn't believe how improved it tasted from the ale to which he and his people were accustomed. "Is this normal? Making drinks from magic?"

Ren laughed. "Drinks and food. Our people don't go hungry or thirsty, although my mother does insist they source food for themselves. We use the ability infrequently with the mortals, but it does come in handy."

"In handy? Never having to wait for the kitchens to serve you food would be a blessing."

He chugged the rest of the ale then wiped his mouth on his sleeve. He imagined his mother's face at the action and wiped a bit slower out of spite. She had always been a stickler about manners, and ever since Xali had been named queen, he'd enjoyed being out from under her demanding eye. It helped that she'd left with Xali's father, the awkward run-ins in the palace no longer something he had to dread.

"I assume you didn't come here simply to conjure me a refreshing mug of ale or to discuss yet another ability that makes my family far inferior to yours."

"No, I did not," Ren said, his mood slightly darker. "And I don't know that Xali's abilities or yours for that matter, are far less than ours. You're both still a puzzle to us."

"Xali has always been a puzzle."

"Always?"

"Yes, even as a child. Never falling into the norms of the family. Her birth occurring strangely and years after it should have, and then there were the moons. The night of her birth the moons were the color of your mother's eyes. I'll never forget the way the green coated everything in its path. I know now it was some link to this Mother Fate as you call her, but at the time, it was worrisome. That's when our uncle began to stir up talk of an omen. It only got worse as she aged."

Ren was pensive, taking every word and absorbing it.

"When did her magic emerge?"

"That was a family scandal," he said. "I may need another fill of ale to go through that."

Ren obliged, and Carnick took another sip, thinking back on their younger years.

"You see, all of us were born with magic…except Xali. There was nothing there. She was like an empty vessel. It further marked her, but it also hid her. My uncle fought to have her killed when she was born, but after it was apparent she had no magic, he dropped his insistence. Over the years, there was a trickle, she could move a few pebbles, sand, or dirt, but that was all. It was as if the magic that had filled our veins and obeyed our commands wouldn't listen."

"She was using the wrong commands, it didn't hear her," Ren said. "But her magic did emerge. When?"

"I don't truly know, nor does she. When I think back on it now, there were always small signs. The way the flowers seemed to reach to her, the way the wind swept by her, pausing to stir her hair. The world reacted to her, but none of us realized what it was and, thankfully, most didn't notice. Right before we woke you, it seemed to burst forth, as though it could no longer stay hidden. The weather unleashed a torrent upon us, snow like we'd never seen well past when we'd expected it and further south than it ever spread." He paused, now seeing how she had truly impacted the weather before the immortals had returned. He ran his hand over his face then took another long drink. "Gods, she influenced all of it and never saw it."

"Fates," Ren said, shooting him a look. "And if those powers had been submerged, never heard for all those years, then yes that's exactly what would happen. Xali is strong. I can sense it when she's present as can my parents. There is much potential within her that still lies untapped."

"Is that why you're here today?"

"Yes and no."

Carnick didn't want to hear the reasons for Ren's visit; the serious expression on his face didn't leave him optimistic. As he listened to Ren's thoughts on his power, he wished he hadn't asked.

"So, I'm not tied to the nature magic like Xali is?"

"No, I'm afraid not. At least, not in the same way. It's there, like an undercurrent to your Dark magic, but it isn't the dominant force, the one driving the outcome of your actions. The Dark is doing that in you and your family. In you, I believe it's heightened. Perhaps as part of the grand scheme, part of the Fates' doing, or perhaps because you were meant to awaken us with Xali. Whatever the reason, the two of you are opposite versions of each other. You with the Dark as the lead and the nature as the follower, Xali with nature as the dominant force, the Dark the tide it rides."

"Damn, this just keeps getting more convoluted, doesn't it?"

"Welcome to life with the Fates and the prophecies they weave."

Carnick stared into his ale. "Xali is the key, isn't she? There is a reason her magic is different, a reason the nature drives her power."

"I believe so. She is the one who will return your line to what it was meant to be, a blend of nature and Dark that contains the beauty of the Elvin magic and the power of the Dark."

"Distinct from us, just as she always has been."

"Are you surprised?" Ren asked.

"Nothing about Xali surprises me anymore. With her, you learn to expect something unique, something special that continues to set her apart from everyone around her."

He thought about what he'd just told Ren, knowing that was how he'd always felt. Amazed by everything she was, enraptured by her beauty, her strength, her spirit. He loved her for all of it, and not even death itself would change that hold she had on his heart.

Xali shifted, the queen having told her to focus on finding Carnick like she had focused on her garden. She appeared in the courtyard instead of inside the palace where she'd expected she would. Carnick jumped, spilling his ale in the process. He was seated on the stone edge and shot her a look.

"Gods, Xali!"

"Sorry," she said sheepishly.

She heard laughter and turned to find Ren seated on the edge of the wall to the right of Carnick. Xali hadn't seen him there.

"I see you've finally mastered shifting," he said through his laughs.

"I don't know if I'd quite call it mastering. I managed to anger your father earlier by landing where he and your mother were."

"So, I heard. It doesn't take much to anger my father, so don't take it personally. My mother says you were meant to be there today."

"Yes, that's what she said, but it really was a simple mistake."

"I've come to find that there are no mistakes."

He stood and stretched, exaggerating his already overpowering stature. "I should be going. Paige is likely growing irritated by my extended absence."

"Does she anger easily as well?"

"Ha, no, but you certainly don't want to be on the end of it when she is angry. She's pure Cirillian with the temper of a Tenebron. Good nigh, Xali, Carnick."

He shifted, leaving them alone. Xali was wondering at his quick departure when Carnick stood, wiping the remains of the spilled ale from his pants.

"You certainly know how to make an entrance, don't you?" he teased.

"Sorry," she said again. "Why did he leave so quickly?"

"He's been here quite a few hours, Xali."

That piqued her interest. "Doing what? Have you been training again?"

His eyes evaluated her as if he were seeing her for the first time.

"Carnick?"

"It would seem there is no more training for me."

"Why not? You just need to tap into that other part of you. I know you can do it, Carnick."

He smiled and brushed back the hair that had slipped to her face. "No, Xali, I cannot. They were wrong. Or at least they think they were. Your power is distinct, ours has morphed through the generations, the Dark power corrupting the Elvin."

"Corrupting it?"

"That's what they think. It's too heavy, influencing our magic, that's why you can do the things you do. Why the ground doesn't rupture when you use your magic. It is you who they think needs to tap into the Dark within you so that it stays more present, enhances your gifts but not overtaking it like it has ours."

She furrowed her brow, trying to understand this new direction. "But why would my magic be different? Mine has always been weaker."

He wrapped his arms around her, guiding her closer.

"No, Xali, your magic is stronger, I've seen it in action. They think your magic is what ours once was but eons of hate for what the Fates did to our people let it reshape our magic and bury that special tie you have with nature."

"That sounds crazy, you know."

"It sounded more convincing coming from him," he replied, laughing.

"So, what does that make me?"

"A first of sorts, a return to who we should have been. When our child is born, he or she will be what we once were…" His words drifted, and she watched as the storm in his eyes grew a light gray. "It's not you…it's us."

"What do you mean?"

"They couldn't figure out why I lean so far to the Dark magic, why I was able to wake them. I favor the Dark blood, you favor the nature, the Elvin side of our magic. Maybe it isn't that either of us needs to open ourselves to anything different because—"

"This is how we were meant to be," she finished for him, finally understanding. "Our heir will return us to our true state, the balance between the two."

They stood there, the weight of the words heavy upon them both. His eyes grew concerned, his mood changing.

"We need to keep you safe."

She bristled slightly. "That's where you go after that revelation? Why should you not be kept safe as well? If we are both meant to produce the heir, we are of equal importance."

He kissed her nose. "I do love it when you get irritated."

"I'm serious, Carnick."

"Because I'm more levelheaded than you."

She pushed away from him and crossed her arms.

With a laugh, he said, "It's true, Xali. You don't think before you go, you let your curiosity, your emotions, your instinct drive your decisions, and that is risky."

"Says your levelheaded over-cautious self."

"Exactly." He moved back to her, brushing his fingers along her cheek. "Your curiosity is one of the things I love about you, but it also puts you in danger at times. You leap in, never looking back or forward to see where the ripples of your motion will fall. That scares me."

"That's who I am, Carnick."

"I know, but as you will one day hold my child in your arms, and now hold my heart in your hands, I won't take a chance of losing you."

She relaxed, knowing he was being sincere and not insulting her.

"You look tired, let's get some rest, who knows what they have in store for us in the morn."

He pulled her close again, and she relaxed into his embrace, breathing in the smell of him, reveling in the strength, the confidence he carried that she admired so much in him. As his lips found hers, she wondered about their life together. A child seemed so far in the future—so many things could happen before that time.

"Want to share what stole your attention from that seductive kiss I just gave to you?" Carnick asked. "It was meant to bring you to our bed, not to push you further from me."

Laughing, she replied, "Simply wondering if we should be practicing for the day we conceive our child." It wasn't a complete mistruth, but as he searched her eyes, she knew he could tell it wasn't the entire truth.

"Mmmhmm." He cocked his brow, a sly grin taking form, one she remembered from their past, the innocent days when the weight of their people's future didn't fall to her. She missed those days, missed that grin. Kissing him, she pushed the present aside and let herself return to those days.

"Mmmhmm," she mumbled, playfully nipping his lip.

"I'll accept that answer and propose that practice is exactly what we should be doing. Practicing more frequently even."

He scooped her up and made his way to their quarters, his lips never leaving hers.

Ren stared out the window of the great library, his mind a flurry of thoughts. Paige, who was curled up beside him, her head on his lap as she read, put her book down and looked up at him. He could feel her eyes and try as he might to pretend he didn't notice, he couldn't and dropped his sight to her.

"I can't enjoy this book if you're stewing up there."

He pushed the book down to read the title, which was hand-written and faded from time. "The history of Dark law. And you think it's me that is to blame for the wandering of your attention? I'd beg to differ on that one. Where did you find such a tedious book anyway?"

She scowled. "Keary suggested I read it."

"Ha! Keary had fun planting that in your head, and I'm sure he'll have even more fun when you tell him you read it."

She stuck her tongue out at him and slammed the book closed. He couldn't help but laugh as he leaned down to kiss her forehead.

"You should know better than to heed Keary's advice, Paige."

"Not going to tell me why you're still fretting about things out of your control again?" she asked, ignoring his teasing.

"My father would say it is because Dark kings don't like things that are beyond their control."

"And your mother would counter that you are not a Dark king."

"Aye, but my father and my uncle would argue that the Dark king in me detests that idea."

Ren, his mother's voice called, taking his focus from Paige.

Mother.

Find me, Ren, there is something you need to see.

Yes, Mother.

He refocused, and Paige sat up, knowing he'd been talking to someone. The fifty years they'd been married was enough time for her to know his ways.

"Who?" she asked.

"Mother, she needs to see me."

Paige nodded. "Go, Violissa comes first. If she called you, then it's important."

He took her hand and kissed it then kissed her. Her hands rose to his face, where they lingered as she pulled back to look at him. "Come back to me, Ren."

He knew she didn't mean physically, that he'd been distant since they'd awoken, lost in thoughts of the ascension and the future of Xali and Carnick. His mind was unable to shake the feeling that all of it was connected and that something more was coming.

He placed his hands on hers and brought them down.

"It will work out, Ren. It always does."

"But at what cost, Paige? We've already lost ten thousand years, our world is a mess, the world I'm inheriting. Our people on the brink of extinction, our land torn asunder. We're rebuilding it all."

"Just as your parents did when they returned from finding each other. I was there, I was by their side as they rebuilt it all, freed the people, restored the kingdom, and I will be by your side as we traverse this challenge. Every step, I will be here. Together, we'll make the kingdom what it once was."

Her optimism brought a smile to his lips. It was one of the things he loved most about her. She was right, his uncle had devastated the lands and their people, his parents restoring it all. They'd faced challenges far worse than this and conquered them.

"You know I love you, right?" he said, drawing her closer.

"Never a doubt in my mind. I didn't wait eight thousand years for you to be born if I didn't love you. You sure did take your time this lifetime."

"And you sure are a heck of a lot older than I am," he teased.

She kissed him then whispered, "Not if you count your first lifetime." She bit his ear then said, "Go find Violissa then return to me, and I'll show you all the wonders age can bring."

"That's tempting. How am I supposed to concentrate on my mother with that thought in my mind?"

She hopped up and grabbed her book before walking away.

"You'll find a way. Meanwhile I'll be boring myself with Dark laws while I bide my time. Quite a turn on."

He groaned, dropping his head in his hands as she left the library. He could hear her giggle as it echoed down the hall.

His mother was waiting for Ren in the lower levels of the Cirillian castle. Ren looked at her curiously upon arriving.

"Interesting place to bring me, Mother," he said, greeting her.

She kissed his cheek, her emerald eyes shimmering in the pale light of the light sphere.

"Where are we? I don't think I've ever been here."

"You haven't. There was never a need, never a reason for us to return. In fact, your father and I thought it lost once the Hidden Realm was freed."

His eyes were drawn to the wall behind her. Intricate Elvin writing lined it, etching deep within the stone.

"This is the entrance to the guardians' lair?"

He'd heard of it in the stories of their past but never had he imagined seeing it.

"Yes."

"Why?"

"It called me. There is something the Fates wish to show you. Only the Fates allow entrance to the lair. Place your hand against the etchings. In the past, it required both your father and me, but I suspect now it is only you who is necessary."

He placed his hand against the stone, surprised at its warmth. He trusted his mother and did so with no hesitation. There was a tingle against his skin then he felt a prick, the etchings filling with light as his magic bled through them. Violet lit their path, growing brighter until the wall shattered, crumbling to the ground then transforming to a thick mist that spread before him into an opening.

He peered back at his mother. Smiling a sad smile, she said softly, "This is your path to follow. I may not enter with you."

Giving her a small nod, he turned back to the entrance, knowing once he entered, there would be no turning back. He stepped through, darkness engulfing him as he heard the wall behind him reform, closing him off from his mother.

Light spread upon the space he'd entered, and he looked up to see clouds opening to reveal the moons. Their light cast a glow upon the scene before him. It was as his parents had described, ruins of the garden his mother loved so much, lost in time. But this wasn't her garden, it was his grandmother's, hidden to protect the prophecy, to protect his mother as an infant until his father had been born. It was just as he'd imagined, and he wondered at its stasis. Why had it not changed when his mother had released the realm from its spell?

Skimming his fingers along what looked to be the remains of

the fountain, he took in the shades of gray, the muted tones that this world held. His parents had stood here once as a key to their destiny had been revealed, a pocket of time that held pivotal moments in the prophecy that had led to his birth.

A cloud floated by the southern moon, the light fading until it covered both the moons, eclipsing him in darkness. He felt no fear; the Dark in him would not allow it.

Silence surrounded him, and his eyes were drawn to a golden glimmer on the wall of the garden. It snaked its way down and across the wall, brilliant golden light that formed writing that blazed in the darkness. His eyes followed the Fates' magic until the entire space was engulfed in gold that shimmered across his skin.

The place that had once guarded his parents' prophecy now held a new one, his path entwined with Xaliandri's. His eyes took in the words in ancient Elvin that were quickly fading, his grasp on the language only minor. The words he did recognize engrained themselves in his mind. Strife, loss, war. He turned quickly to the ending that was blending to the darkness. Unite, he recognized, anew, then finally, the last line held his eyes until it too disappeared into the dark.

The clouds parted, the moons casting their rays upon the muted space, the entrance crumbling to allow him exit. He had seen what he was meant to see. Slowly, he walked out, the doorway reforming as he approached his mother. She was wringing her hands, her bottom lip sucked in as she chewed it, her now sage eyes filled with worry.

He took her hands as she eagerly awaited his news. She knew, her instinct guiding her that this was the Fates calling him to claim his role in the prophecy. He nodded, and her eyes grew watery. She above all else understood the importance of prophecy, knew that he would need to accept it or face dire consequences as she and his father had.

"It is done," she said shakily. In that moment, she looked almost frail. A weariness was upon her, one he'd never witnessed but one he knew stemmed from the constant plague of prophecy that had ruled her life. His mother was the strongest woman he knew, the strongest in their world. She held the power of the Fates themselves, but for that moment, she seemed a vulnerable, frightened mother, tired of a battle to please the Fates, having sacrificed everything, including him at one point.

He brushed her loose curl back as he'd seen his father do countless times.

"It is done. There is no turning back, the Fates have spoken, my path has begun, intertwining with Xali's as we suspected…" he hesitated to tell her more. "The culmination of the prophecy that defined you and Father."

"You were always the end of our prophecy, our journey completed so that you could take our place and finish whatever it is the Fates are seeking."

"Aye, but this time, it ends with me. Well, with us. Xali is on this journey, and there is no turning back from what she's started. Carnick is part of this as well."

"And what is it she has started?"

"The end or the beginning of everything. The final outcome rests upon her."

Nine

Half a moon had gone by, and there had been no word from Xali's father or Carnick's mother. Xali was growing nervous and Carnick with her. It didn't help that Ren had kept his distance as well. It left them both restless. Carnick watched as she went through her training exercises, the sword always her way of focusing, leaving the rest of the world out. He took in the graceful moves, the fluid motion of her muscles, she having donned a sleeveless tunic to allow her better movement. She was strong, and it was her strength that he loved.

It seemed just yesterday he was going through those moves with her, carefree, unburdened, worried only about taking the throne one day, dreaming of having Xali by his side, in his bed. Now that had all changed. She was by his side and in his bed, but she was queen, he second to her rule. In his younger years, that would have bothered him, but now…now he had changed. She had changed him with her curiosity, her tenacity, her strength. At some point, he'd relaxed his concepts of what it meant to be first or second born and brought her to his status in his mind.

He wondered what would have happened if he'd never changed. Would they be here today? Would she still be in hiding? Would any of it even have happened? A first born would have squashed her talk early on, stifled her spirit, clamped down her curiosity. Forced her to conform from the beginning.

Had he been different, she may have been as well. She may have remained safe.

Xali took another set of dancelike strikes at the air. Her target was false but her aim true, and he knew any living creature on the receiving end would have been downed quickly. If he had tamed her the way his mother had always wanted, would he have loved her as deeply? It was her spirit he adored, the same spirit that had led them here. He shook his thoughts from his head, smiling as he commented, "I do believe you have thoroughly slayed that ray of sunshine."

Smoothly, she flung the sword to the ground and turned to him, a smile on her face.

"Chose to break free of the palace confines today, I see," he said, moving closer.

She was outside of the palace but still within the gates, respecting the wishes of the immortals that she stay protected until her powers were mastered. The palace gates were lined with the best soldiers from his army and her father's.

"I wanted some fresh air."

He laughed at the absurdity of the comment, knowing most of the palace lay open with plenty of fresh air.

"Are you sure you're not simply escaping me?" he said, bringing his finger up to wipe away a smudge that lay on her cheek.

"Never," she replied, the storm clouds in her eyes growing thick.

"Well, well, Xali, I can oblige to cooling you down, but you may need to rinse yourself first. As much as I'd love to ravage the warrior that you are right now, you do stink."

He playfully kissed her nose then touched the sweat that gleamed against the hair she had pulled back from her face.

"Ah so your desire for me hinges on my cleanliness?"

"Very much so today," he replied, laughing.

"There was a time you would have taken me anyway, regardless of my state."

"But now I can have you any time, and although I do love when your skin beads with sweat, I prefer that sweat be from exertion with me."

She laughed, kissing him. "I suppose I can oblige, a hot bath…" her words were cut short as they heard "Rider!" from the guards at the front gate.

Carnick tensed, not knowing if Xali was the rider's intended target.

He listened until he heard, "He wears royal colors! Lift the gates!"

Xali relaxed, but Carnick remained tense, moving to stand before her.

"Carnick, I can protect myself."

"I will always stand guard before you, Xali. That rider approaches swiftly. What if he is falsely wearing our colors?"

They had kept the royal blue of their family to honor their heritage but had added an edge of forest green to show distinction from the original family colors and to acknowledge the nature powers that Xali had come to claim. His mother had wanted to add the gold of their house, but Carnick had denied her request. Theirs was a new reign, one no longer divided by houses, the blue would stand as the only acknowledgment of their family's past rule.

Carnick watched as the rider approached too quickly, without hesitation, without slowing. His senses rebelled, and he threw up his hands, calling his power, the land screaming in response as it tore from its resting place and billowed, sending the horse to the ground, its rider forward, rolling until his body came to a stop.

"Carnick!" Xali screamed in reaction.

"We don't know who it is, Xali, and we are to trust no one."

As the rider tried to rise, his hood slipped back.

"Fates, it's Mendol!" she yelled, running to her brother who had collapsed back to the ground. The guards were running, alerted to the commotion, weapons drawn, but Carnick gestured for them to stay back.

He ran to Xali's side. Mendol looked pale as he gasped for breath.

"What have you done, Carnick?" Xali asked.

"It's not what I've done," he replied, moving the cape further back to reveal the blood-stained tunic.

Xali brought her hand to her mouth in shock. "Mendol, what's happened?"

"Treason. Aunt Hastrial and Katama they…they've turned against you. Father is gone, dead." His words came out strained but clear enough for them both to hear their message.

"No, no, that can't be. Mendol, you're delirious," she said, but Carnick knew that was denial talking. Mendol was mortally wounded, he could only be speaking truth. Their suspicions had been right.

Fear gutted him. "Mendol, where's Fairenth? And my mother?"

"We hid Fairenth. Trevant has her, they're hiding with Ainia."

The second borns, all in hiding with only one first born…all in hiding except Xali. His nerves tingled, nudging him to get her to safety.

"Your mother is wounded, they have her held prisoner," Mendol said weakly, redirecting Carnick's focus.

"Why isn't she fighting back?" His mother was the strongest of the heads after Xali's father. But then, they'd cut him down.

"They did something to her and Father. Their magic lost while they fought. They were powerless."

Carnick couldn't move. Xali's father gone, his mother powerless and wounded. He looked to Xali, her distress evident as the wind whipped around them. Thunder roared, and dark storm clouds encompassed the sky, so thick they almost appeared to touch the ground.

"Xali, contain your power!" he yelled against the wind.

The storm in her eyes was vicious and black, the green specks flashing like lightning within them.

"Get him inside safely. Get the immortals to heal him, they'll know what to do. Find Ren, he'll fix Mendol." She was rambling, having risen then backing from him with each word.

Carnick stood and grabbed her shoulders. "Xali, calm yourself. We'll figure out what to do. Let's get Mendol healed first, then we'll get Ren's help."

Her expression hardened. "I don't need his help. They will pay for harming my family, for killing"—her voice broke, and his heart fractured for her—"for killing my father."

"Xali, don't be rash, they will pay, but you don't have the strength to fight them. If they rendered your father and my mother helpless, they would do the same to you."

A streak of lightning tore through the sky, a crack of thunder shaking the ground, and then she was gone.

"No, no, no! Xali!" he screamed although he knew she was nowhere close, knew she had shifted to enact revenge, shifted to her death.

"They'll kill her," Mendol wheezed out.

"I know." And there was nothing he could do to stop it.

Xali landed on the furthest shoreline of the new land. The waves pounded against the surf, the sound lending her no comfort. Her aunt Hastrial had erected a massive palace along the crest of the land where the shore met the grass. It towered over her, leaving her shadowed from the morning sun. She'd been instructed to live in the house they'd built for her. A modest home, the same as had been built for her aunt Katama and uncle Lengan, and for her cousins. A palace was only reserved for the queen, and her aunt was no longer queen. Yet here stood her palace, ostentatious and proud, standing in defiance to Xali's command. In defiance of her lack of title. No longer queen yet still behaving as one.

Now, she was no longer Xali's aunt. She had forfeited that title when she had murdered her brother, Xali's father. At the thought, the waves behind Xali rose, crashing with more force. Her breathing constricted as a physical wave of anguish crested within her.

"They must pay," she said, steeling herself to the emotions.

She knew her aunt was waiting for her, along with her other aunt and uncle. All knowing she would come, but would they expect her so soon? It was a three-day journey at least to this end of the new land. Had her father mentioned her shifting ability? Or had he kept the information to himself? She didn't have the answer, all she had were questions, but it mattered naught; she was going in to punish those who had dared harm her family.

When she reached the entrance to the palace, she realized she'd neglected to bring her sword, having left it standing in the ground. The guards drew their weapons, and she cursed herself before remembering she no longer needed a sword.

"Traitors," she mumbled as the ground rose below them, long roots breaking through, entangling their limbs and dragging them to the ground. She may not have mastered her magic, but she'd learned a lot that day with the queen and the Elvin.

Walking past the guards who were now writhing within their root prisons, she willed the land below the palace to rise, crushing the doors to rubble before lowering it. Although she did not have her family's ability with stone, she had other weapons at her disposal. As the last of the rubble fell, she spied Hastrial, waiting for her, arms crossed beyond the opening.

The wind stirred, whipping Xali's face, her loosened strands of hair stinging her. Bravely, she walked through the remains to face her aunt. She wondered what it would be like to have the king's power, to kill without movement, to inflict pain at her will. With that thought, something deep within clawed at her, begging to be set free and she did so, feeling the Darkness climb, feeling it weave through the nature, the two merging.

Embrace the Dark power within you, Xali thought, Ren's words coming back to her. Part of her fought against it, remembering what Carnick had said, the Dark had overtaken the nature in her family, warping it to what it was today. Her power was supposed to be the lighter side, the gentle side, but she didn't feel like being gentle, she wanted to see pain inflicted on her aunt and those responsible for hurting her brother and killing her father.

Hastrial's expression changed, hardening in reaction to whatever the Darkness had done to Xali.

"You killed my father, wounded my brother, and Carnick's mother. Now, you will pay."

Hastrial smirked. "You haven't changed one bit, Xaliandri. Still the same second born wishing for power, wishing to be like the rest of us. But you never will be. You will always be the outcast of this family, the one who should never have been. We should have killed you at your birth like my husband wanted. He knew, knew you were a scourge, a plague on this family, and you were."

Her words were like venom, slinking into the wounds within Xali's heart and grabbing hold. The Darkness breaking just enough to give her pause.

"You were always weak, why my brother let you run free was always beyond me. Your mother softened him, and you ruined him."

The Dark flared at the mention of her father, and Xali roared, the foundation of the palace quivering, slabs of stone rupturing below their feet. Her aunt never moved, continuing to stare at Xali.

"You murderer!" Xali screamed, running toward her, wanting nothing more than to strangle her.

"You treasonous little brat!" she screamed.

Something hit Xali with a force that sent her sprawling. She landed hard against the now uneven stone floor, her rib taking the impact against the edge of one slab that had been left uprooted from her outburst. Pain tore through her as she yelled in agony, feeling the shattering of the bones. She tried to pull herself up, but the pain left her breathless. Something ripped through her skin, something that gripped her, searing her from the inside out. A cry escaped her. She tried reaching for her power, but it didn't heed her command; something had it locked away where she could no longer grasp it. She was powerless. Rolling over, she found her remaining uncle, Lengan, standing over her with both her aunts.

"It's time we do something about you, niece, time to make you pay for daring to turn on us," Hastrial said, grabbing her roughly. "Time to make an example of you, foolish child, and then we will finally do what my brother should have done the day you were born."

She didn't need to ask, she knew what they would do. Her mind flickered to Carnick. Why hadn't she listened to him? He'd warned her, he'd said they should get Ren, but she hadn't listened. And now she would die before he could make it to her. She would die, a victim of her own pride, her stupid foolish emotions. She would die and never see him again, never feel his touch again. All that they'd fought for would be lost.

As the guards picked her up, the lingering pain from the loss of her magic and the piercing ache in her broken ribs leaving her immobile, she pictured Carnick's face until it faded, blackness taking over.

Ten

Staring at the space where Xali had been, Carnick cursed, feeling helpless. She was gone, shifting recklessly without a plan, without him, with no protection.

"Carnick," Mendol said in a strained voice, "where did she go?"

"To them," he answered. "To her death."

He looked over at Mendol, his face strikingly pale, the wound a fatal one that would bleed him to death, slowly over a few days. He'd already journeyed three days at least; his time was short. "Take him inside, alert his mother. Find someone who can stay the wound longer," he commanded the guards.

"Where will you go, sire?"

He looked to the west, his heart wanting to follow her. He would never make it in time and would lose both Xali and Mendol. She'd made her choice.

"To the immortals to get help. They're the only ones who can save Mendol, and maybe then we can save her."

He ran, leaving them, praying Mendol would survive. His mind was only on Xali and finding a way to get to her in time. He felt helpless, out of control, and the feeling wasn't welcome.

Time dragged as the stablemaster readied their fastest stallion.

"Carnick!" He heard his father's voice, frantic as he called to him. "Son, what are you doing?"

The stable hand brought the stallion out, and Carnick quickly mounted, hands holding tight to the reins.

"Getting help."

"Let me come."

"No, they won't trust me if I'm not alone."

"Then let me ride to the others. Find your mother and Xali."

"No!" he said quickly. "Don't. We've already lost Uncle and perhaps even Mother. Do not add yourself to the list. If they outpowered him and Mother, they will do the same to you."

"Being second born makes me no less than them."

"I know, Father, but they are hunting us down. Striking at those they consider traitors, and you are among them."

"She's my wife, Carnick. As miserable as she can be, I still love her."

Carnick saw the sincerity, the pain in his father's eyes.

"I know, but she may already be lost and Xali with her. Stay here please. Fortify the palace, stand guard here in case they strike before I can return. Here is where I need you."

He nodded, accepting his assignment then said, "Be careful. Bring them home."

Carnick kicked the horse and fled, not wanting to further delay the trek, knowing that every minute he lost brought him closer to Xali's and Mendol's death.

Xali tried lifting her head, but everything hurt. Her entire body was on fire. Her chest ached, her breathing was labored, and her ribs throbbed intensely. Slowly, she forced her head up against the pain and tried to focus through the dark that surrounded her. Her eyes adjusted a fraction, and she spied a torch in the distance, well past the bars that caged her. Bars that surrounded her prison, black and gnarled from the power that had formed them. Her hope faded the more she stared at them, knowing she had made herself a prisoner the moment she had chosen to ignore Carnick's pleas, the moment she'd let her emotion decide her path. Pulling herself to a sitting position, she couldn't contain the cry that escaped her as she straightened. She leaned against the cold stone wall, trying to catch her breath, to make the waves of pain and anguish that were overwhelming her disappear.

After a few moments, she dragged herself across the floor to the bars, feeling for any weakness, sending her power out to call to the land. There was no answer—as if it no longer existed. She could still feel it deep within her; it simply ignored her call. What had they done to her power? What were they planning to do to her?

She looked up to see if there was any opening to her prison, but the bars spread from the floor to the cavelike ceiling where they ended. She knew the truth, had seen the dungeons in her father's palace. They were formed from the magic of her family and were unbreakable, except with magic. Magic which she could no longer access. Magic which she'd never mastered, the abilities of her family always foreign to her. If she'd had her magic, could she have even broken through to her freedom? Dropping her head, she leaned against the cold bars, her mind wandering to her father, wondering if he'd suffered before his death, if he'd been here in this empty prison awaiting his death as she was. What had she done?

"It's no use." She heard a weak voice. "Even if you had your magic, it's not enough."

"Aunt Renia?" she said, raising her head then crawling toward the voice only to find bars on every side of her.

"Yes, child. You can't escape. You should not have come. Your father thinks…thought you special, a sign from the gods, a way to finally rid our family of the cursed lies. He was wrong. You fell the moment they drew you here. You should have stayed safe with Carnick. You have doomed yourself, doomed him."

Xali felt the tears burn her cheeks, thankful that her aunt couldn't see them. She tried to see into the cell, but it was too dark. All she could make out was her aunt's shape on the floor. Labored breaths could be heard then her aunt spoke again, her voice a whisper.

"Your father is dead, his life forfeited for supporting you. Now, I will lose my life for standing by his side. Your brother is dead—"

"No, he found us, he's…" She paused. Was he safe? She remembered how pale he'd looked, how he hadn't risen. Had she doomed him with her rash decision? She could have shifted to Ren or his mother, could have saved him, waited to confront the others. But she hadn't, and his death would be on her hands.

"He will die, and you will be the cause, just as you are guilty of your father's death and mine. You should never have lived. We should have listened to Crebant and killed you the day you were born. You should have left them to sleep. You are no savior, you are a plague…" She was struggling to talk, coughing what sounded like liquid.

Blood, Xali's mind explained, and she could taste the bile in her own mouth. "You are an abomination, and you will be the death of us all." Her last word was drawn out with a heavy breath that lingered until there was nothing but silence.

Xali scooted away from the cell bars, pain lacerating her side with the movement. She ignored it, too afraid to stay near her aunt's dead body. There was no need to check to see if she still breathed. Xali had heard the rattle of her chest as a final breath had escaped. She felt the loss of her spirit, the emptiness that accompanied her death. She sobbed, the weight of the words, the loss of her father and possibly her brother burying her. She wretched with the force of her tears, the pain unbearable with the shaking of her body, but she couldn't stop. She pulled her legs in and laid upon the cold floor, missing the warmth of Carnick's embrace and praying to the Fates that they would take her from this nightmare.

Carnick had journeyed for two days, taking minimal breaks, driving the stallion until finally its legs collapsed under it. He was thrown as the horse fell to the ground, its body lathered in sweat, its breaths rapid and labored. He would go no further, having run the beast to the ground.

He looked around. Stranded, in the middle of nowhere, no towns close by, no means to reach the immortals. Two days had passed, and night had set on this one, the last rays of the sun sliding under the horizon. How was he to reach Xali? To save Mendol? Every hour he lost was one which might steal them away, steal her from him. He dropped his hands to his thighs and tried to steady his breathing as panic set in.

Rising, he let out a scream, his power slicing through the open land, ripping it from its resting place, sending it rising in a ridge across from him. Wiping his shaking hands across his face, he tried to wrangle in the emotion, to think rationally, but thoughts of Xali's death kept him from his task.

"Well, well, we have a stray in our borders."

Turning, he found the king's brother. Even in the dark, his pitch-black eyes could be seen accompanied by the sneer on his face. Carnick pulled himself together.

"I was sent to discover why there was a rush of power here, and it seems I've discovered the source. Why are you in our land?"

He crossed his arms, awaiting Carnick's answer.

"I need to find Ren or his parents. We need help. Xali…her father has been murdered, her brother gravely injured, possibly my mother. Xali went for revenge, and I fear they'll kill her if I don't get to her."

The brother raised his eyebrow. "Well, that is quite a conundrum. Your family is turning on one another, killing each other one by one, and you want me to stop it. I could do nothing. Let you all kill one another, and we'd be rid of your lot like I wanted in the first place. I could tell my brother, who is pestering me at this moment as to why there was a disruption, tell him it was nothing and be done with you."

Carnick's heart beat rapidly. He'd never imagined they wouldn't help, but why would they? This would be their chance just like the brother said. This was their world after all, and Carnick's people were invaders. He wanted to plead but somehow knew that would make matters worse, that these men respected strength, showing no weakness. So, he remained silent. The brother glanced at the horse that lay dying.

"Ruined a fine beast," he said, putting his hand out and squeezing it. Carnick heard the horse's neck snap, his body stilling. It had taken seconds and barely any movement for him to take another life. Carnick stared in awe, wondering how many lives he'd taken.

"Plenty," the brother responded as if knowing his thoughts. He looked back at Carnick. "Be glad I'm no longer the bad guy. If you'd met me in another life, you'd already be dead."

He grabbed Carnick's arm roughly, and the world disappeared. His feet hit solid ground, and he tried not to stumble as he met the king's eyes. They were black as the room, even the light sphere seemed to be pulled into their depths.

"Carnick, what's happened?" the queen said, running over to him. Ren appeared from nowhere and Carnick jumped, still not steady from the effects of the shift. He felt suddenly lightheaded and swayed slightly. A few other men joined them as the room spun.

"Tynan, help me get him to a chair," the queen said. "He's exhausted."

"Where did you find him again?" the king asked.

"About a hundred miles into Tenebron."

"It looks like he hasn't slept in days."

"I'm sure he hasn't based on the tale he's told me. I warned you, Ren. Your father and I both did. They would cause trouble, turn on her and force our hand. And that's exactly what they've done."

A tingle swelled through Carnick, cool and light. Within seconds, he was refreshed; the exhaustion, the hunger, the thirst from the past two days now erased. The fear, however, lingered.

"That's enough, Tynan. Ren and I both know your opinion. Now let the boy talk," the queen snapped.

Boy. She'd called him a boy. He should have been offended but given their age, he supposed he would be a mere boy.

"Carnick, what's happened?" she asked softly.

He recounted the events, the direness of the situation returning with that feeling of impending doom. "We need your help. Xali will die, her brother, too, if he hasn't already succumbed to his wounds."

The queen stood. "Cody, go to the palace, heal her brother if you can. Eoin, go with him in case there's trouble there already."

They nodded then disappeared.

She looked to her husband, and a few moments of silence ensued before the king spoke.

"Ren, we'll leave the next step in your hands. You will be king in less than a moonspan, and their continued existence was your call."

"Yes, Father."

"I don't think it wise to engage them, Ren," the brother said. "As much as I'd like to see them all done away with."

"Tynan's right," the king agreed. "There's something off about this. Xali can shift, she should have come to us by now. Either she's dead, or they've done something to her powers. Bound her perhaps?"

At his words, reality sharpened its knife again and plunged it into Carnick's heart. Dead. Could she really be dead? The thought had crossed his mind, but he'd pushed it aside, clinging to the hope that she was still fighting.

"Ren, can you sense her? I can't find her," the queen said.

He shook his head. "The connection is no longer there, but that doesn't mean she's dead."

"True, we must have hope."

"Do you think one of them has that spell? The one Drakine used on us?"

"No," the queen said. "Even if they do, their bloodline is too diluted now to wield it. But that doesn't mean they don't have the ability to bind their own kind." Her eyes locked on Carnick. "Do they, Carnick?"

"I don't know what that is," he answered honestly.

"A king may bind or restrain the powers of his Council or even blood in some cases."

"I remember that distinctly, brother," Tynan said, "on two occasions those damned chains ground their way through my flesh. Not the most pleasant experience."

"It was for me." There was no humor in the king's voice, and Carnick involuntarily shuddered. What was it their past held that would have led to the king finding pleasure in his brother's pain?

"If she's still alive, we have limited time to save her," Ren said.

"Is it our place to save her?" the brother asked.

"Why wouldn't it be?" Carnick asked, surprised at how heartless the man had sounded.

"Because you are not our concern. Drakine forced his way into our lives, disrupted them. We no longer want your disruption. My nephew has an ascension to prepare for, the rest of us are trying to spend our last days soaking in the flesh of our physical existence. Your kind is an irritant that will not go away."

"Uncle," Ren said, the brightness of his eyes changing to a rich navy. "It is not our place to let Xali die. She is here for a reason, you know this, her place in the prophecy clearly aligns with mine."

Prophecy? Ren's words surprised Carnick. They were confident, there was no question in them this time. Had he seen the actual words, seen Xali's name among them?

"So, what does he do?" the queen asked.

"He helps Carnick save the girl, then enacts punishment on the guilty ones," the king said.

Punishment…death. His family had guaranteed their death. He should have felt remorse, some sadness, yet he didn't. Instead, he was ready to strike them down to save her. Every last one of them.

Eleven

Light pierced the darkness, stinging Xali's eyes. She heard the cell open then hands grab her, rough and jarring. The pain seared through her side again as the splintered ribs were awakened. She let out a cry, the hands forcing her head up. Weakness flooded through her limp body. She didn't know how long she'd been in the dark dungeon, her only company the body of Carnick's mother. Had it been mere hours or days? Time was lost to her.

"Are you enjoying your stay?" Hastrial asked. "I see my cousin didn't make it. Shame, she was strong, would have made a good ally."

"Ally?" she wheezed. "You're not in a war."

Her aunt grabbed her face, her nails digging into Xali's cheeks, drawing blood.

"Make no mistake, this is war. You declared it when you turned your back on us, when you woke those monsters and gave them our land. "

"It was never our land to take, and you know it. We stole it."

The slap came quickly and viciously. Xali felt the remaining sting, her skin growing hot. The sting woke her, the pain of her injury searing through her body, every nerve screaming.

"Lies, all of it lies. You are a disgrace to this family, a traitor, and tonight, you will die. Bring her."

Xali tried to struggle despite the pain, knowing she needed to break free, knowing what lay ahead of her if she didn't. She kicked and flayed, punching one of the guards before his fist met her jaw. She tasted the blood, her lip splitting before she fell hard on her broken ribcage. Screaming in pain, she could do nothing as the guard kicked her. Waves of agony crashed through her as the foot met the shattered bones. She fluttered in and out of consciousness, the dungeon disappearing, a staircase flashing before her, followed by glimpses of a palace. Why did they have a palace? She couldn't remember, her memory hazy. Blackness again encompassed her vision.

She floated in the darkness, letting it take her, welcoming it in place of the despair and pain. If she were to die, this would be a fine way, lost beyond the physical reality. She let it take her, like a warm embrace that encased her. It would be easy, the world would go on. Would the immortals punish them? She thought of Carnick, and the darkness became less welcoming. Would he miss her? Mourn her? The thought of his touch forced the darkness to recede further.

A sudden rush to survive overtook her, a need to awaken, to live, to see him again, feel his touch, taste his kisses. She ascended through the darkness, grabbing all of her will. Her eyes flew open with a scream that tore through her.

She fought the guards, instinct taking hold, something deep within calling to her. Vines climbed their legs and pulled the men from her. She ran, disregarding the pain, the setting sun casting long shadows on the ground before her. They'd brought her outside, presented a way for escape. For a moment, hope was imminent; they didn't seem to notice she had escaped. The palace gates weren't too far. If she could just make it, then she would be safe.

The ground burst open before her, and she stumbled, landing hard on her side. Spikes of light flicked across her eyes with the glaring pain. She stared at the gates then crawled over the torn ground.

She heard the tear of the land before it burst forth below her, sending her through the air, another rupture making sure she met a sharp crest as she descended, the wind knocked from her. Before she could catch her breath, it bucked then burst open, and she was mid-air again. Over and over, her body was thrown, landing hard upon each impact, bringing more pain until finally she landed at an awkward angle, her leg breaking from the impact.

She cried out, her hope long gone.

"Fool. You can't run, you are powerless, and today, you die."

"Even if you kill me, you won't win." She forced out the words, each one tearing from her like claws of agony. "The immortals will hunt you down and punish you."

Hastrial lowered herself so that Xali could see her.

"They won't win. We defeated them before, we will defeat them again."

"How could you kill him?" she asked. "Your own brother."

"My brother turned traitor the minute he stood up for you and those murdering immortals. He was no longer my brother."

"But you're a second born," Xali wheezed out.

Her aunt squeezed her broken leg, pain flaring through her, another scream escaping.

"My husband is dead. There is no first born left in my line."

"Your daughter—"

"Is a traitor as well. Hiding the other second borns. I would have made her queen to rule alongside her cousin, but she chose to harbor your brother and his bride. They will all die now."

"And you will lose. If you kill all the children, there is no one left to rule, to continue what it is you're fighting for."

"There's one," her cousin Sartria said, stepping forward. "And Trevant will abide my command."

Xali stared at her cousin. "Trevant is a second born—"

"Who is currently locked away with my treasonous cousin. I will find him, and he will have no choice but to follow my command. We're joined and trust me, I can manage to get an heir whether he cooperates or not." Her eyes held a dangerous glint.

"Let's get this over with," her aunt Katama said, the only head of the houses that remained. "Kill her and be done with it."

"The immortals will kill you," she said defiantly.

"No, they won't. They'll be too busy fighting. We have something special in store for them. Not all of the Fates as they call them were happy with their choice to let us live. Not all are content with the meddling of one Fate and her pets. Now, they will all pay."

Fear ebbed its way into Xali, not for herself, for she knew she would die, but for Ren and his family. They were powerful but could they fight the Fates themselves?

"What have you done?" she whispered.

"We're about to unleash the fury of the gods upon this world. And you, my dear, are the sacrifice. Do it," she commanded, rising.

Her uncle Lengan dropped to her side. "I'm sorry," he mouthed.

"Uncle, please don't do this. Please."

He shook his head sadly and pulled out a knife and a vial. Xali backed away, her broken leg convulsing with pain, dragging limply along with her. Fear reared within her, thunder rumbled, and the ground creaked.

"I thought you bound her power?" Katama asked.

"I did," Hastrial replied.

The thunder was Xali's; there was something left in her. She called to what she could, praying she could save herself. Roots erupted below Hastrial, grabbing at her, clawing her face, and wrapping around her.

"Do it now!" Katama screamed.

"I can't, Katama," Lengan said. "I won't be part of this anymore."

The ground rose, but he blocked it—not before a sharp stone pierced his head, sending him to the ground in a sudden thud, the same sound the stone had made upon contact with his skull.

"Can't rely on filthy second borns," Katama grumbled, grabbing the knife and twisting it into Xali's chest before she could react. She held the vial up and let Xali's blood fill it as Xali cried for her to stop.

Standing, she looked at the vial with a sadistic smile.

"Time to call the gods home." She threw the knife to the ground then pulled Hastrial from the vines. "Enjoy your slow death, traitor. They won't make it in time to find any breath left in your treasonous body."

Xali struggled to breathe, knowing Katama had hit a fatal spot within her.

"You won't make it," she wheezed, the metallic taste of blood on her tongue.

"You think you're the only one in the family with lesser powers," Hastrial said, wicked scratches along her cheeks from the roots. "You're not." She grabbed Katama and Sartria then disappeared.

Xali's head collapsed, her eyes registering the moons high above her. So, her aunt could shift. She absently wondered what other lesser powers she had and how none of them had known. Why would that not have connected them? Why not embrace Xali if they were the same? Because they weren't. Shifting was a Dark power, and all Xali had sensed from her aunt was Darkness. She didn't have the Elvin magic, the softer side of their power. She only had the Dark, and it had turned her and any sanity she'd once held.

Weariness overcame Xali, her mind slipping to Carnick, missing him, worrying for him, his fate. Would they kill him, too?

The metallic taste in her mouth made her gag, but she had no strength to move. She was dying. Her aunt had fatally wounded her, stolen her blood and left her to a slow death. She coughed, blood slipping from her mouth, but she couldn't move to wipe it away.

Why had they needed her blood? They were calling the gods? Was that what her aunt had really said? Or were they calling the Fates? She'd said some of the Fates were angry. Were they helping her aunts? Gods. She had used the old term but previously used the word Fates. Why the distinction?

Her mind was growing fuzzy, her vision hazy, her eyes staring blankly at the sky. Death was on the horizon, coming for her. Her aunt had made sure to leave her just on the cusp of death, to drag out the pain, the relentless fear of knowing her last breaths were being taken. As she lay there, her breaths raspy with blood, a breeze touched her skin.

For a moment, she wondered if it were the Mother Fate coming to take her away or perhaps the queen finding her. But then it grew in force, whipping her hair across her face. Lightning tore through the sky, and thick black clouds overtook the moons, stealing away the light. She lay in the dark, her eyes growing heavy, her fight to breathe weakening. As her eyes closed, she thought of Carnick, a final tear drifting down her cheek.

The room was silent as a gale howled against the windows. Ren was listening as was his mother. It had come from nowhere, and as the moons were shielded by heavy black clouds, he felt his mother touch in his mind.

Do you sense it, Ren?

Yes, Mother. It's something unnatural.

You need to find the girl, now," his father commanded, even he noticing the sudden change. Addressing Carnick, he continued with, "What have your people done?"

Appearing confused under the heavy concern that rested upon

his face, Carnick asked, "Is she still alive?"

Ren sent his senses out, feeling for the other powers in their world, brushing past the Councils, out toward Carnick's family. He found the few in Xali's palace, and then out further to the very edge of the lands, he found more but not the ones he needed. These were the ones in hiding, the cousins to Xali; he could sense their fear. But where was Xali? She had a distinct aura from her family, lighter with her nature magic. He'd been trying to sense her as they'd been talking, but each time, he'd been blocked, something dark was shielding her from him and he couldn't breach it. Even if they had somehow bound her power, the trace of nature should have still been there. He scanned again, and this time found her, a faint aura, quickly fading.

"Yes," he said hurriedly, "I've found her. She's alive but not for long. We need to hurry."

"Go, Ren, bring her here once you've healed her," his father said.

Ren grabbed Carnick's arm and shifted, praying the Fates hadn't claimed her, for once they had, even his power would not bring her back. They landed outside, the sky a frenzy of lightning, the storm decidedly worse this far west.

"Where is she?" Carnick yelled over the wind.

Ren threw a light sphere out, the darkness of the storm making visibility nearly impossible.

"Gods," Carnick said as they took in the wrenched land that had been ripped and shredded across the courtyard where they stood. Ren saw something, running only to discover the body of a man, the back of his head caved in, the heavy stone still wedged in his remains.

"Uncle Lengan," Carnick said, moving to the body.

Ren grabbed his arm. "He's gone, we need to find Xali, fast. I can only sense a dim aura. She's fading, and if the Fates have claimed what remains of her, I cannot heal her."

"What? Why not?"

"It is against their rules. Once they claim a soul, it is beyond our power," he yelled over the wind.

Carnick's face dropped as rain fell upon them. "Then let's find her."

They spread out, moving up and through the piles of land and debris, the wind tearing at them. Ren rounded a corner and saw a small hand, the rain washing the blood away.

"She's here!" he screamed, running to her.

She was in poor shape, her wounds intense.

"Fates," he muttered, dropping next to her.

"No!" Carnick screamed, stumbling over. "You can heal her, right?" Ren heard the desperation in his voice.

He sent his magic out, feeling for the deeper injuries, feeling for the Fates who waited in the wings. They were close, he could sense their presence, but they had yet to claim her.

"I think, but I need to do so quickly," he said, calling his magic and sending it slowly into her body. With deeper injuries, healing was best done slowly else the patient would die from the invasion of magic, the force of it destroying them from the inside out.

He pushed through the surface injuries, the broken bones, past the fracture in her spine far into the rupture in her lung. As he reached it, he felt her slip further, the touch of the Fates closer.

Mother, he called to her in enaigne, *I need you, she's too close to death.*

His mother appeared, dropping down immediately, her eyes meeting his, knowing exactly the severity of the situation. The touch of her magic met his, and they both began to work.

"Shouldn't we move her inside?" Carnick asked, the rain coming harder.

"No, she'll die if we move her, there's not time," Ren answered curtly, irritated at the intrusion on his focus.

His mother's magic weaved through the wounds with his, delicate, gentle, methodical. She knew the risk of rushing just as he did. When they'd healed her lung, they moved to her spine.

"Keep her out, Ren," his mother said. "If she wakes during this, it might harm her."

He sent his Dark magic to Xali, casting a sleeping spell over her. Meeting his eyes, his mother sent him a smile.

"Why are your eyes violet?" Carnick asked, jarring him once again from his concentration.

"Because all three of my powers are active, the healing through my Light, the storm triggering the nature, your interruptions my Dark side. Now stop interrupting before I put you to sleep, too," he gruffed.

He's curious, Ren.

He's disturbing my concentration, Mother.

You're just like your father.

Sometimes.

She smiled again, her eyes sparkling.

"You finish the spine. I'll heal her leg," she said.

They continued, Carnick pacing in the background until all the injuries were healed. Ren sat back and relaxed, breathing a sigh of relief. The worried expression on his mother's face, however, eradicated the relief.

"She was bound," she said, affirming their suspicions. "You should be able to lift it."

A strike of lightning lit the night sky, dangerously close.

He moved his hand in a wave over where Xali's core lie, feeling the bindings, loose and easily undone, sensing the power return to her.

"Are you ready to wake her?"

He understood there was more to the question, his mother's instinct evident in the crystal emerald in her eyes, for waking her meant finding answers to the torrent that currently engulfed them. One which reeked of unnatural elements and something that disturbed his own instinct. His father's words echoed in his mind, *what has your family done?*

Fear pummeled Carnick along with the rain and wind. He hated the feeling that now ravaged him. Xali lay lifeless as Ren and the queen sat beside her, a glow of bright blue encasing her body. Healing magic.

He paced, interrupting them on two occasions and hearing the irritation in Ren's voice, his violet eyes never looking from Xali's body. His answers did nothing to alleviate the curiosity or the fear. Why had his Dark magic been called? Was it really only Carnick who had brought it to the surface, or something else? There was a feel to the air, something thick, ominous that nudged at his own power, pulling at it, urging it forth. Was it the same for Ren?

Stopping his pacing, he looked at Xali. When they'd found her, his heart had fractured. He'd never seen her look so weak, so fragile. She was caked in blood and dirt, the rain washing it away, her skin so pale she looked as if death had already claimed her. She'd seemed so vulnerable. He wanted her healed, wanted to hold her, to feel the rise and fall of her chest against his as she drew healthy breaths, wanted to hear her voice, see the emerald specks of her eyes.

Time seemed to stand still as they worked, his anxiety rising with each raindrop that fell. His anger stirring at the acts of his aunts. He glanced back over to where his uncle's body lie. Had he tried helping Xali? Was this the payment he had received? Had his wife been the one to make the fatal blow or his cousin? Mendol had distinctly left Sartria from the list of those in hiding, only stating Ainia's name. Had she killed her own father?

Carnick had no doubt Sartria was by her mother's side. She'd always been a greedy one, obsessed with power. In their younger years, she'd shared her desire to be in Carnick's bed, to be his betrothed rather than Trevant's. He'd been tempted to take her offer, to bed her prior to her joining with Trevant. She was seductive, a temptress who flaunted her body to have her way. He had turned her advances down, knowing if Xali ever found out, it would crush her, and he would never do that to her. She was the only one he truly wanted; Sartria offered nothing in comparison to Xali.

After denying her, he'd discovered that she'd even pleaded for her betrothal to be changed, that she be given Carnick instead, but a first born could never join with another first born and so her final attempt had been squashed. Angry, she'd turned her bitterness to Xali. It was never obvious, only small things, but Carnick noticed, hearing the remarks, seeing the actions, the way she would always needle at her, reminding Xali of her shortcomings. It had been relentless until Carnick had finally confronted her, stopping her action with a few threats of exposing indiscretions of which he'd been made aware. Ones that would harm her standing in the family, weakening her future position as queen.

Carnick turned his eyes back to Xali, impatiently waiting until finally, he saw the color return to her skin, her breathing grow steady. His tension withdrew, relief taking its place. Ren and his mother sat back, and he heard the queen ask if Ren was ready to wake her. Carnick remembered Ren threatening to put him to sleep. Did they have that ability? Was that part of their Dark magic, the reason it had been present?

He watched as Ren waved a hand over Xali's head. She inhaled deeply then coughed, the sound one of choking. The queen rolled her gently to her side, and she continued coughing, blood spewing from her mouth with each cough. Each cough feeling like a knife slicing Carnick's heart; it ached to see her this way.

Finally stopping, she grabbed the queen's arm. The queen moved her hand, and the blood on Xali's face disappeared. She helped Xali sit up slowly.

"We healed the damage, but the remnants were still within you," she said softly.

"I'm not dead?" Xali asked in disbelief.

"No," Ren answered, helping her stand.

"You'll be sore, your body in shock from the injuries and the healing, but you're alive."

"I thought I'd died, I didn't think…thank you," she said quietly.

"Thank you both."

She gave Ren a hug, then the queen.

"Just be glad I'm not my father or he would have laid you back on the ground for daring to touch him. Besides, we only deserve some of the credit. Without Carnick, you would have been lost."

Her eyes met his, and Carnick's heart repaired, sputtering to life at the warmth of her gaze. "Carnick," she said, before trying to run to him. She stumbled, and Carnick ran to catch her.

"Careful, that leg and your spine are going to be a bit shaky until the trauma dissipates," Ren warned.

"I'm here, Xali."

"You are. I…I thought I was lost to you."

"You almost were," he said, brushing her rain-soaked hair back.

"But how? How did you reach me?"

"The fool found us. Nearly killed himself and did kill a fine stallion I'm told."

"You traveled to them? But that's days. I don't—"

"Shhh. I'll tell you the tale in due time," he said, lightning tearing across the sky. "Now, we need to get inside, and you need to tell us what's happened."

"Yes, yes, I should. Oh, Carnick…your mother…she's gone."

Carnick's spirit dropped. He'd forgotten she was here, his mind only on saving Xali. He pushed back the emotion and nodded. It was something he'd have to come to terms with in time. They both would, her father had been lost as well as the uncle they'd both lost. So many lives. Was this the price they'd paid to wake the immortals or was this only the beginning?

"We need to go," Ren said, approaching them. The queen was already gone. "I'm sorry about your mother, but we have to get back now."

Carnick didn't have time to respond before the world disappeared, replaced in moments by a warm, expansive room. A massive table sat in the center, twenty-two chairs posted around it, two elaborately carved chairs at the heads. Tapestries lined the walls, histories of times past, stories he'd never known but was keen to discover once this was over. At the far end of the room, a large fireplace burned, its glow casting shadows through the room. Windows lined the outer wall, the storm battering them with extreme force.

The Dark king stood at the far end, the queen by his side, the brother leaned against the wall, his arms crossed, a leg propped behind him, glaring at Carnick. Others stood throughout the room, while yet others were shifting in. The mood was serious, the atmosphere heavy, dense.

Xali grabbed him, and he realized she was shaking.

"Father, Uncle," Ren said in greeting as Carnick moved Xali to the closest chair.

A few of the men raised eyebrows, and he noticed an uncomfortable silence.

"That chair belongs to my queen," the uncle said gruffly.

"Tynan, it's all right. This isn't official, and she's still very weak," the queen replied, her voice seeming to calm the room. A wave of warmth drifted across Carnick, and he realized the rain had been dried from his skin and clothing. Xali was now dry and clean as well, as fresh as he'd seen her the day she'd left.

"It's nice to see you're safe and alive, Xaliandri," the king said. "Although my brother would say otherwise."

Carnick cast a glance at the brother who still wore a scowl.

"I need you to tell me what happened to you, Xaliandri," the king continued.

"Are you up to it?" Carnick asked her, squeezing the hand he still held.

"It doesn't matter if she's up to it. The world is in chaos at the moment, and her situation cannot be coincidence."

Anger swept through Carnick, the emotion of the day, his weariness, the loss of his mother and uncles, the near loss of Xali, pushing him past his limit. He stood, hands clenched.

"She's just returned from the brink of death," he said. "You will not command her to do anything."

A vise gripped his throat, and Carnick struggled to breathe. He kept his eyes locked on the brother, aware that he was watching for hesitation.

"I will command anyone I want to whenever I want," the brother snarled. The room grew dark, the flames of the fire turning black. "You are only alive because of my brother's good graces. You will respect us, or you will understand why I was once known as the most vicious Dark king in our history."

"Enough, Tynan," the king said.

The vise released, and Carnick gasped to recover the air he'd lost.

"You need to learn to hold your tongue, boy, or Tynan will take it."

He felt Xali's hand on his arm. "It's all right, Carnick. I can tell them."

He looked back at her, taking in the storm clouds where specks of emerald fluttered. "Please forgive him, he's just trying to protect me, as he always is," she said with a small smile.

"Maybe you should heed his protection next time you rush into danger," the brother retorted, surprising Carnick.

"Please tell us what happened, Xali," the queen said, her green eyes now a rich sage.

Thunder broke through with a fury that shook the room. Xali flinched, and all of them turned to the windows as a large tree sailed through the glass, shattering it in every direction and pouring rain inside.

Instinctively, Carnick raised his hand, turning the glass to sand as Ren's magic turned the tree to ash. The ground rumbled below them, and the queen grasped her husband's arm, nearly falling.

"Vi," he said, catching her as Ren and his uncle ran to her side. The others moved closer, the mood of the room turning.

"I'm all right," she said softly. Her eyes, now a blinding emerald, met her husband's, whose were filled with worry. "The land has been riven, in northern Tenebron, somewhere near the mountains."

That's why she had fallen. Her tie to the land physically affected her. The king moved her to what Carnick assumed was his seat.

"Keary. Eoin. Find out what's happened. Someone fix that window."

Two men disappeared while Carnick watched in amazement as the window was reformed. There was no substance it was pulled from, like his magic needed. Instead, it simply was there again. It was the same way they'd rebuilt the castles and everything within them, creating them from thin air. Once again, the depth of their power left him awestruck.

"I need to know what's happening," the king said, "and, Xali, you are the only one who knows."

"I don't know, that's the issue. I can only tell you what happened to me."

Xali glanced around the room, all eyes upon her. She should have taken time. Time to adjust to being alive, to being healed. Time to fathom what had happened to her, to let it sink in. Time to mourn her father, her uncle, her aunt. Even with the vile words she'd spoken upon her death, she had still been family. Part of a family that had betrayed her, tried to murder her, despised her. Although her aunt hadn't been the one to draw the final wound, her words had left a scar.

They continued to stare at her, awaiting her words, thinking she had answers that she didn't. She only had questions. Regardless, she began to talk, letting it spill out, wrenching a fresh wound in her newly healed body with each word she relived.

When she had finished, the room remained quiet. Carnick's hand was still holding hers, his fingers tightening with each abuse she had received. He looked devastated, the color drawn from his face, a face that reflected the emotions that stirred within her.

"I'm sorry about your mother," she said. "I tried to reach her, but…but she wouldn't have let me help her even if I could have."

Storm clouds swirled in his eyes, and she knew he understood the reason. The change in his expression was swift, the clouds sparkling with violet specks.

"She was a bitch," he said. "Family, tradition first. It was she who called the heads to punish you that night. She would have been second in line to execute you after Uncle Crebant. Always complaining that she'd been tricked into joining me with you. Never satisfied with knowing I loved you. Never trusting that I could lead as well as she. It's better this way."

He turned from her, dropping her hand, lost to her in memories, both good and bad of his mother. She had yet to dwell on thoughts of her father, and as the king spoke, she pushed them aside once more. It was too hard, the pain too fresh to let it in. The situation too concerning to break her fragile façade of strength. She was one tear away from breaking, and she couldn't allow that. She was even too afraid to ask about Mendol, fearful that he had not survived and that those words would destroy her.

Sometime during her story, the two men who had gone to inspect northern Tenebron had reappeared. No words had been spoken, yet she knew the king had answers as to why the queen had fallen. Apparently, they weren't answers he would be sharing.

"Do you know where your aunts went?" the king asked.

"No, Katama only said that not all the Fates were happy with your decision to let us live. She said she was going to unleash the fury of the gods upon this world."

"You mean Fates," the brother said.

"No, she said gods. They were two distinct references."

He looked at the king, silence ensuing as if they were talking to one another.

"Sinow, what's happened to the land?" the queen asked.

"It's been ripped open like you said but not by any magic that we know. The mountain is spewing flames like a volcano, the far western edge collapsing into the ocean. The land below the ocean has risen to meet it. Even the Torathar island is now connected to our land."

"Island? What island?" Carnick asked the question in Xali's head, although she also wondered what a volcano was but refrained from asking.

"It's a piece of rocky land, uninhabited that sits miles from the coast, too far to reach or even see," the brother said.

"It is part of our past, one we thought long gone," the queen added. "Do any of you feel the culprits?"

"No," Ren answered. "I feel four near their palace where we found Xali, but that's all."

"The cousins, Fairenth," she said. "They were hiding, afraid the others would strike against them."

"But we feel no others, so why is that?"

The king began pacing.

"The same reason I couldn't sense Xali. Something was blocking me, shielding her presence," Ren answered.

"Something powerful enough to avoid detection by one of us does not bode well, brother."

"No, it does not," the king said. "Whatever it is, it's only shielding the culprits and those nearest them, which is why you couldn't detect Xali until they'd fled."

"What if they go after the others?" Carnick asked. "My sister is still there."

"Daneele, Benon, go to the others, make sure they are healed if need be and bring them to Xali's palace," the queen instructed. "Cody is still with your brother, Xali, and what remains of your parents." Her sage eyes held the sadness Xali carried in her heart. Relief weaved its way through her body with the knowledge that Mendol was alive.

"Darkbearers, hunt the guilty ones down. Bring them to me," the king commanded. "I want every inch of that land scoured."

No words were spoken. The men in black disappeared, all pulling capes over their heads before they shifted, two in white capes departing right after.

"What remains of my Council, please check the towns through Tenebron to ensure the people are safe," the queen added.

"And Cirillia?" one asked, his bright blue eyes matching those of the others and Ren.

"Yes, once Tenebron is secured, head there. We don't know how far the storm has spread, but if we feel it here, Cirillia is bound to be impacted."

They disappeared, and Xali and Carnick were left alone with the royal family, the king continuing to pace.

"It's nudging at you as it is me, brother."

The king stopped pacing. "Why differentiate? If her family calls them gods, why use Fates?"

"One would only do so if they believed in the Fates," Ren said.

"Which they do not."

"Unless they now do," Xali said absently.

"Could they have interchanged the word?" Carnick asked.

She thought back to that memory, hearing the words again. "No, they were deliberate."

"Xali, your people have always believed in the gods?" The queen's sage eyes lightened, the emerald fighting for dominance as a faraway look overtook them.

"Yes, that's the only recorded history that goes back to our beginnings."

"And what does that history say? Is there any mention of the Fates?"

"No," Carnick answered. "Although Xali's brother is the scholarly one."

"Yes, you're right. If anyone knows, he would," Xali said.

The queen looked back at her husband, and within moments, one of her men appeared with Mendol.

"Xali! Carnick!" Mendol went to run to them but was grabbed by an unseen force.

"Reunions later, we need answers," the brother said.

A pained expression was on Mendol's face until he took a step back, the brother's grip loosening.

"Tynan," the queen said.

"We need answers, Violissa."

"He's right, Vi. Tell us the history of your gods, boy," the king said, crossing his arms over what Xali now noticed was a massive chest. She took the three of them in, the king, his brother, even Ren. They were an enormous presence in the room, physically and magically. That sense of overwhelming wonder settled over her again.

Mendol looked as if he wanted to argue the term boy but thankfully refrained. "What is it you're looking for?" he asked instead.

"Any reference to our Fates," the queen answered.

"Only that they are heathen gods, that our gods were the true gods, the first gods."

"The first gods?" Ren asked.

"Does that notion go back further than the history in our lands?" the king asked.

"Well, yes. As far back as the beginning. We don't have history of our people further back but writings on the gods we do."

"And how does it say your people were created?" the queen asked.

"That's always been the strange thing. There is never any reference to that, only to the gods themselves, their claim on this world, that they were the first. The writings began at a time when our people were developed, passed on orally before that."

"The first gods," the brother repeated.

"What if the Fates weren't the first," the queen mused softly.

"But the Fates created us, Violissa. We know that as a fact."

"Aye, and they created Xali's people. You confirmed that," the king added.

"Yes, but what if they didn't create this world? What if someone or something else did?"

Her words hung in the air, and a chill shivered through Xali. She didn't know why. She'd always known the gods, they were part of her upbringing. She'd been forced to worship them at the shrine, although her faith in them had never been as her family's had.

"The shrine," she said. "It had images of men—"

"False images. Imaginings of what your gods would look like, nothing more," the king said.

Rising, the queen walked to the window, the storm shrieking just beyond it. "If the Fates stole this world, if they buried its creators—"

"Time to call the gods home," Xali repeated her aunt's words.

"Wake the gods," the queen corrected. "They've been dormant just as we were."

"Waiting for someone to wake them," the king added.

"Feeding on the prayers and worship of your people for eons. A people abandoned by the Fates, refusing their own creators out of spite. Leaving an opening for persuasion from a false god," the brother said.

"No, a different god. This isn't a war between us. This is a war between the gods and the Fates. They've woken the enemy of the Fates, and now the battle has begun." As the words left the queen's mouth, the castle shook, thunder booming so loud that all of the windows shattered with its force this time, the sky beyond alight with fire and the white remnants of lightning streaks.

Twelve

"Come to bed," Paige said, her soft hands wrapping around Ren's waist as he stared at the storm outside.

"I don't think I can sleep. I should go back."

"Your father sent you to get some rest. Your mother is doing the same, and I'm certain he's with her. Now, come to bed."

She was right—no one knew what to do. This was beyond them, beyond their power. If his parents were correct, only the Fates could solve this. He'd brought Paige to his parents' home, unwilling to be away in case anything happened. It was better that they all be together while they figured out any kind of solution. He'd situated Carnick and Xali down the hall, thinking it best as his family had, that they remain under protection, particularly Xali. She had enemies, ones who had nearly killed her, had murdered her father and Carnick's mother. Her own family trying to kill her.

He thought of all the times his uncle had tried to kill his parents and him. It was a strange feeling to know someone you loved had tried to kill you and those you loved. His uncle was changed now, redeeming himself over countless centuries, but Xali's family was still out there plotting her demise. Thunder shook the castle's foundation. Plotting the demise of their world if it hadn't already begun.

He couldn't comprehend the thought that there had been others here before the Fates. If that were true, had the Fates been the usurpers once, just as Xali's family had been? Had they torn these lands from other beings, ones who had truly been the creators of this world? The idea destroyed everything they'd known about the Fates. It seemed as though the same events that had brought Xali to awaken Ren and his family were now playing out on a grander scale. To what end? Would these gods war against the Fates? How would they survive such an occurrence? He'd never seen the Fates, only been told by his parents what they appeared to look like. They'd always appeared in mortal form, the same stature as their children. Would the gods appear the same? Or would they be the nightmare he imagined them to be?

He ran his hand through his hair and sighed, the storm crashing outside.

"Ren." Paige kissed his back, returning him to the present. He took her hand and squeezed it, knowing she was right; there was nothing he could do now, nothing any of them could do.

"You win," he said, "but I can't promise that I'll sleep."

He turned to her, the cerulean eyes he adored shining up at him. Pulling her in against him, he rested his face in her hair, taking in the strawberry scent that lingered on her, remembering the first time he'd noticed it, the first time he'd seen her.

"I don't know that we can fix this, Paige."

"You and your parents can fix anything. I've seen Violissa and Sinow conquer challenge after challenge, and they've always won."

"With heavy battle scars."

"Yes, but they won, and this time, they have Tynan on their side."

Pulling back to look at her, he said, "Always the optimistic one, aren't you?"

"Someone has to be around here." She kissed him. "Now, let's get some rest so you can help them solve this in the morning."

He acquiesced, and sleep took Ren even though his mind fought it. He opened his eyes, expecting to find Paige in his arms, the warmth of their room on his skin. Instead, there was only a vast emptiness. He was standing outside, the air thick with Darkness and something else he couldn't pinpoint. Snow was falling around him, but no cold touched his skin. The thick fog before him dissipated as a cloud cleared from the moon. He stared up—why was only one moon visible? Then he realized the moon before him wasn't complete; it was only partial, the remains of what had once been the female moon, the edges jagged where she had been gauged. Thick particles of light floated to her right, and to his terror, he saw that they sat where the male moon should have been.

The snow thickened, sticking to his skin. Dragging his eyes from the shards of the moons, he put his hand out, the flakes thick and warm, not melting in his hands. He brought them closer, their consistency that of ash. Bringing his eyes back to look before him, he held his breath as the fog broke, and he saw that it was actually smoke. Before him lay a world unknown to him. No trees lay upon the barren land, no fields around the surface. A land of ruin and decay had assumed its place, violently filled with black stone and abrupt mounds that spewed fire and lava.

He turned, looking for anything, anyone. He heard the screams of his people but saw no one as souls were imprisoned somewhere past his vision. The air smelled of sulfur, smoke, and death.

No sign of the world he knew remained, no sign of his family, his friends. At the thought, the ground rumbled, the air exploding around him. He was thrown back, the abrasive surface tearing at his skin, but he took no notice as his eyes drawn to the sky. Glimpses of gold and silver flashed against black and red—the Fates, the true Fates and the gods. He had no doubt this was the remains of their war. Several Fates fought a flurry of what he assumed were the gods. But where were the rest? Pulling his eyes from the battle and the gold and silver dust raining upon him, he surveyed the land again, his heart freezing as he saw the bones, massive bones that still sparkled slightly below the black surface. *The remains of the Fates*, his mind screamed. He scrambled over, digging into the rough surface, frantically trying to reach the fragments. As his hand touched a sparkle of silver, the knowledge of the Fate filled him. He dug and dug, then brushing against the gold, he sensed they were remnants of the lesser Fates, those taken by the true Fates once they'd returned their lives, called upon to fight by their side. Both the true Fates and the lesser Fates lay buried below him, lost, defeated by the old gods of this world.

He fell back, anguish filling his soul. They would lose. Whatever Xali's family had begun could not be undone, the end was upon them. Ash covered him in a thick coat while his eyes drew back to the battle, but it was frozen in a stasis that allowed him to see the sheer beauty and power of those remaining Fates. The ash hung in the air, stillness surrounding him. No sound to be heard.

The ash stirred, and a voice filled his head. *It is time, Ren. Only with your parents can this fight be won. You must take the crown, you must let them go so that we all may live.*

Her voice washed over him, and in the distance, the Mother Fate stood. Her thick silver hair hung loose, her green eyes glowing gold rimmed through the haze. Her size was towering, leaving him feeling small, inconsequential in the grand scheme of their world, and he stared, awe-struck.

It is your time as it is theirs. Have hope, for all is not lost. You will be tested, as will the girl and her mate. The three of you on the path. Your parents now called. Let them go so that the final steps may be taken. As she spoke the last word, a gnarled black hand grabbed her, tearing into her waist, silver spattering as blood would before she was ripped from his sight, the emerald of her eyes fading along with her presence. A roar shattered the silence, and Ren woke with a sudden jolt.

"Ren? Are you all right?" Paige asked.

He lunged from the bed, throwing on his clothes and tearing from the room. He heard Paige calling behind him as she tried to catch up with him. He ran hard and fast until he slammed into someone, falling with a graceless tumble.

"Dammit," he growled at Xali.

Her eyes were wild, and he knew without question she'd been there. He stared at her as Paige and Carnick caught up with them.

"What's going on?" they both asked.

Ren ignored them and grabbed Xali's hand, knowing she was part of this event. Fear raked through him, a fear of impending loss, of the unknown, of the future he'd seen. The image of the Mother Fate's destruction still in his mind.

He tore through the halls until he reached his parents' room. Throwing open the door, not caring if it angered his father, he came to a halt as he met their eyes. They knew. They were standing in each other's arms, a stoic expression upon his father's face.

His uncle shifted in with Chastity, his face reflecting Ren's emotion. The oldest of the Councils shifted in as well, Keary wringing his hands.

"No," Paige said, her hand flying to her mouth as she ran to her father, Daneele, the eldest and only remaining of his mother's Council. The others had all moved on before the long sleep as new Council were called for Ren's reign. These were the last to return, the ones who had sworn to stay until his ascension, until his parents returned to the Fates.

"It is time," Ren said, repeating the Fate's words.

His mother nodded, her eyes glistening.

"The Fates have called us," his father said.

"Well, isn't this an unprecedented quandary," his uncle said. "Here I thought we'd have at least the final moon."

Ren could hear the sadness in his voice, his uncle's hand

clenching Chastity's tightly.

"You're leaving," Xali said. It wasn't a question, more of a statement.

His mother looked up at his father, bringing her hand to his cheek before responding. "This is Ren's fight and yours. Our time here is complete, our part in this world done."

"But I haven't ascended yet. How am I to rule without…"

The wind blew the doors of the balcony open, the rain halting, static in the sky as the ash had been in his dream. The clouds broke open, and he was compelled to walk out, a breeze drifting upon his skin gentle and warm. He tilted his head to the sky, and closed his eyes, feeling the tingle of magic that grew, layer upon layer, first Dark, then Light, then nature until he could almost take no more from the force of it.

He opened his eyes, seeing the world before him from a new perspective, sensing the weight of each raindrop, the Darkness that layered each storm cloud, the touch of Light the moonbeams held in the slivers that cut through the clouds. He breathed in, a sudden weight upon his head. His fingers reached up to touch the crown that now adorned his head, the crown he would now wear as king of their world, the one that had awaited his ascension.

Turning, he found his father's eyes filled with pride, his mother wrapped in his arms, tears upon her cheeks.

"And so, we have an ascension," his uncle said, the same pride in his voice. "Guess that's our sign. No turning back now, eh, brother?"

"Aye, but don't think of choosing a spot anywhere near me up there. Last thing I need is to have you by my side for eternity as well."

"You might miss me too much if I don't."

"You might be right, brother."

Ren couldn't help but smile, knowing how long it had taken his father to let his uncle into their lives.

His mother walked over to Xali, her fingers lingering in his father's until she was too far to hold.

"You can't leave," Xali whispered as if she'd known his mother for as long as the rest in this room had. Perhaps in her own way, she had. They'd shared a connection, and perhaps that's why she was here now.

"Shhh. You are stronger than you know, Xaliandri. You are meant to fight alongside my son. To bring our world together, to right the final wrongs of the Fates."

"I can't do this, you can, all of you can, but I can't."

His mother took her in her arms. "You foolish girl, open your eyes and see what we see. See what your husband sees." She kissed her head. "Only then will you know your true power."

She let go of Xali and moved to Carnick.

"Stay by her side, she will need your strength and your will as well as your magic. You will both be tested. This is bigger than you know." She paused, a look upon her face that Ren had seen before, the one that told him she was seeing beyond the sight of anyone present. Seeing something only she could. "Yes, your paths shall not be easy, they will test you far more than you can imagine."

Her words lingered, and Ren saw the fear in Carnick's eyes, the same that had inched its way forward in his own chest.

"The Fates always have their reasons, no matter how difficult the path."

She kissed his cheek then turned to Paige, Carnick's eyes dropping to the floor, her words having left the three of them shaken.

"Paige, my old friend," she said, taking Paige's hand, leaving the words she'd spoken to Carnick behind like they'd never been said.

"I'm a bit tired of saying goodbye to you, Violissa," Paige said, sniffling.

They both laughed, then hugged.

"How am I to make it without you?" Paige cried, and Ren could feel her anguish, the same that now engulfed him.

"You always have me here." She pressed Paige's heart. "And in my son."

They hugged again then Paige ran to his father who was not the hugging type and embraced him. They shared a history that spanned well before Ren's birth, and it was one that had brought them close. One that had placed her as close to his mother as a sister could be and to his father as any of his most trusted Council.

"Dammit, Paige, you'll ruin my reputation," his father grumbled.

"I'll miss that, Sinow," she replied with a smile, wiping the tears from her cheeks as she backed away from him.

As the final goodbyes were said, his parents came to him.

"I can't face this without you," he said softly.

"You can and you will," his father said, squeezing his shoulder.

"But you…this is too soon, you didn't get your time together, and I…" Vulnerability crushed him, his Dark side rising to cover it as his mother folded him into her arms.

"We've had all the time we're allowed, more than we ever imagined," she whispered.

"All right, Violissa, stop babying him. He's a king for Fates' sake," his uncle said, pulling him from her arms.

"He's right, Vi. It's time to let him go."

"Have fun with the two of them, Violissa," Paige said, laughing through her tears.

"I'm glad I'm not one of them, stuck with each other for eternity, I'll take floating around in spirit form any day over that," Keary joked; he was best friends with Ren's father and had chosen to stay until their return, having been through everything with them. Ren would miss him sorely, jokes and all.

"So how does this work?" Chastity asked, rubbing her arms.

"No one really knows, all we know is what's written."

"Is that normal?" Carnick asked, pointing to the balcony where a glaring white light was glowing brilliantly.

Ren sucked in his breath.

"No," Tynan said.

The light shimmered then a silver sparkled throughout it.

"I think that's our sign," Chastity said. "Tynan…"

Ren watched his uncle with the one person who had loved him—not despite his past but with it. He held her, the Dark in him fighting to hide the vulnerability.

"I love you, my Dark prince," she said as her skin shimmered golden sparkles that spread from the golden specks in her eyes.

"Chastity…no," his uncle said, the Darkness eclipsed by the man Ren knew loved her with every fiber of his being. Ren's heart lurched at the impending loss. She was his aunt. She'd been thrust onto their path unwittingly by the Fates but had quickly become part of their lives, part of Ren's as he had grown.

"Shhh, I'll find you no matter where you are." She kissed him, and Ren watched as she faded, leaving a trail of golden glitter that fell through his uncle's fingers.

A slight cry escaped his uncle before the Darkness shrouded his heart. Ren's father squeezed Tynan's shoulder before they heard Keary say, "I think it's our turn."

Ren didn't think he could take anymore; he was losing everyone. First his aunt, now Keary. His father rushed to Keary and grabbed his arm in the Tenebron brotherly shake as Keary began to return to the Fates. "Keep an eye on him, Violissa, he's going to be a handful for those Fates."

She laughed through her tears. "I think they have more to fear from me."

"My queen, my brother," he said as he dissipated.

His father's face dropped then Paige cried. Her father kissed her head as the shimmer reached his skin.

"Keep her safe, Ren," he said.

"I promise."

"Violissa, Sinow. It has been my honor."

His mother cried through her smile. "As it has been ours." Ren knew they had said their true goodbyes prior, knowing he'd want to be closest to Paige as the Fates claimed him.

He bowed and within moments was gone. Paige backed into Ren's arms as the light filled the room, nearly blinding him.

"Well that leaves us," his uncle said, the Darkness still covering his loss. "Why aren't we shimmering like they did?"

"Because that's not your place," Ren said, thinking back to his dream. "Your place is with them." As he said it, the room was flooded with a silver light. The Mother Fate emerged followed by the two Dark Fates, the three who had decided the destiny of his parents.

Ren made to bow as did Paige, Xali and Carnick not knowing better, but the Mother Fate gestured for him to stay his bow. His mind flickered back to the image of her from his dream and, as if knowing, she gave him a sad smile.

"That is their place, not mine," his uncle said.

"You underestimate your role in the prophecy, Tynan," one of the men said, the sheer power of his voice shaking the room.

His father grabbed hold of his mother, pulling her tight, protectively, a last effort to hold her close.

"Dark child, she is yours. Your son is correct, your place is with us." The three turned and stepped back into the light one by one.

The battle is beginning, Drostiren, the Mother Fate's voice seeped through his mind, referring to him by his full name. *Even we do not know the outcome.*

"Ren," his father said, drawing his eyes from the light.

"Father, Mother."

We love you, his voice echoed through his mind, one last moment of affection which he rarely showed.

His mother looked back at him once more, a golden sheen encompassing her emerald eyes which shone from the tears behind them. She gave him a smile that filled his heart with the love she held for him.

"I love you both," he said, the Darkness reaching up to shield him from the pain that threatened to weaken him.

"No love for me?" his uncle joked as his parents walked toward the light.

"Be brave, Ren, you are the end, the reason for everything we survived, the reason for our love," his mother said as they both paused, their skin shimmering a brilliant silver, power cascading the room as they transcended to their place as true Fates. Chosen to sit beside the true Fates, a blessing bestowed upon a very rare few, most becoming lesser Fates.

"I'll be damned," his uncle muttered, his eyes staring at the place where they'd been, only a slight silver dust in their wake.

"Catch up, brother, before they change their mind," his father's voice boomed.

His uncle strolled toward the light. "Any chance I could get visits from a certain sexy ephemeral spirit while we're there?"

Paige laughed, and his uncle winked at them. "Don't burn the place down in our absence, nephew."

"I'll try not to, Uncle."

He watched as his uncle turned the same silvery shade his parents had before fading away.

The light disintegrated, the room dark, the glitter of silver and gold the only evidence his loved ones had ever been there. He felt Xali's hand on his arm before she and Carnick quietly left, likely knowing no words could allay the endless gulf of emptiness that had taken over him.

Outside, the storm raged once again, rain slashing through the open balcony of what had once been his parents' room.

Paige's arms wrapped around him tight, but his eyes continued to stare at the space where they'd been, tracing the whisps of silver that floated away in the wind of the storm. Paige's tears soaked his shirt, waking him from his trance, and he gripped her small body tightly to him through the quakes of her sobs. Lowering his head, he wondered how he would go on without them, how he could possibly fight the oncoming storm without them by his side.

Paige sniffed then looked up at him, grabbing his face in her hands.

"Don't," she said as if she knew his thoughts. "We knew this was coming. We prepared for it. You have prepared for it, trained for it. You will be an amazing ruler, one to rival your father and your mother. You are the best of them both, Ren. There is no one better prepared to fight this enemy than you."

"I miss them already, Paige. There's a hole there now, one that wasn't there before," he whispered.

"One I carry as well, one we will fill with our love, and eventually the love of our own son."

She kissed him, then dropped her head back to his chest. They remained wrapped in each other's embrace as the storm raged around them until the sun finally rose.

Thirteen

Xali lay in Carnick's arms where she'd been since they'd returned to their room. Carnick held her tight although his breaths indicated sleep had taken him finally. It had yet to find her. Staring at the high ceiling above them, she replayed the events for the hundredth time, still not willing to believe the inconceivability of it.

They were gone, the immortals or most of the more powerful ones, all but Ren. His parents and uncle taken by the Fates. There was no longer any doubt of the Fates' place in this world. No doubt of the power they held. Snuggling further into Carnick's embrace, she pushed back the tears. They hadn't been in her life long, but they were part of it. There was an emptiness, a broken connection now that wasn't there before, tied still to the queen but now severed, leaving a loss she didn't understand.

She thought back, past the emotion of it and thought about the dream. The image of the broken world was one that she didn't welcome back, but she knew was important. She had seen the devastation, the ravaged land, heard the screams and then the battle. It had been too much, the terror of it threatening to drown her. Stumbling forward through the smoke, she'd seen him, Ren. He'd fallen from some force, and she'd watched as he dug frantically.

What was he looking for?

And then she'd noticed the shimmer just below the ground, the golden flecks. As her eyes drew closer, she'd brought her hand to her mouth, stifling the scream. The Fates had fallen, those remaining were losing the battle. The world was lost, the Fates defeated.

Forcing her eyes away, she'd looked back at Ren, seeing the silver figure above him, a golden light surrounding him, beauty in the remnants of chaos. She knew now that it had been the Mother Fate. What had she said to him? Xali hadn't heard, her attention drawn to something on the outskirts of the dream, lingering, watching.

Where Ren had lain in the light, embraced in its strength, the darkness now encompassed Xali, cold slithering its way across her skin. Out of the darkness, something emerged, black and terrifying. It towered over her, casting a shadow even with no light, even with the distance that lay between them.

The hairs on Xali's neck had stood, along with goosebumps that painfully raised upon her skin. She'd tried to breathe, but no air remained, the last of it tight within her chest. Red eyes brimmed with black, the red like the lava that covered the ground, boiling within them. Its body was in the shape of theirs but massive, standing at least fifteen feet, broader than the mountains that had once stood behind it.

Xali had tried to scream, but like the air, it stuck deep within her. The god, for she knew it to be a god, studied her then raked one massive hand at her. She'd cringed, awaiting the blow, but it never came. Peeking her eyes open, the beast, the god, was gone, the world alive with emerald, blue, and gray tones that danced, flickers of red within them. Below her feet, the world exploded, green bursting through.

She'd woken suddenly, knowing what it meant, knowing in her heart they were all connected, she and Ren, his parents, and the Fates. Known the dance of light, the burst of green healing the land had been something unexpected. Something that had been coming for the eons that the prophecy had been in motion, his parents. They were needed, being called to fight the terrifying gods that were waking. There was no stopping their coming, all that could be done was to prepare for the war, to add to their ranks. Perhaps that had always been their course, the prophecy building to this step. She'd only had prophecy and the Fates in her life for this short time, but she understood the complexity of them, the far-reaching impact they had.

That's why she had run, why she'd rushed to their quarters. Ren had known too, known what it meant for his parents, running to them as well.

And now they were gone. She sighed, moving closer to Carnick as the image of the god returned to her mind. It had wanted her, but why? Something told her it wasn't to kill her, there was something more, she simply didn't know what.

"Xali, if you push any closer to me, you'll crush my ribs," Carnick muttered drowsily. "Get some rest."

She turned her head into his chest as his arm tightened around her, praying the image of the god would flee and then wondering who exactly was hearing her prayers.

Morning came quickly, and Xali was roused by a knock on the door. Blinking her eyes open, she realized sleep had claimed her at some point through the night. Carnick had risen and was now standing in the window, the storm incessantly battering at it, no light from the morning sun to be found.

The door opened slightly before either of them could answer it.

Paige's head slowly peeked in, her eyes puffy and red, circles lining her delicate features.

"I see you're up, or perhaps you never slept," she said. "I'm sorry to disturb you, but I thought perhaps you would break fast with me until Ren returns. I could use the company, and I know he wants to speak with you."

"Of course, we will," Carnick said. "Please come in further."

"Xali needs to dress still, I can wait outside."

"Nonsense," Xali returned, rising to show that she had never changed from the prior night.

"Ah."

Xali threw a tunic over her chemise and pulled her hair back quickly.

"So much faster than these dresses," Paige said. "I should speak to Violissa again about…" Her words drifted off, and there was a sudden silence. "That's right," she said absently. "I'm queen now. That will take some getting used to."

"I'm sorry, Paige," Carnick said.

Paige shrugged. "We expected it before the sleep, I don't know why it's so hard now. It feels like the preparation of goodbyes was wiped away with the sleep, and we had to start over again, but this time without the forewarning, without the time we'd expected. And then…then they were just gone."

Xali didn't know what to say, she had yet to even begin her own grieving of her father. As if remembering this, Paige said, "We will have time to grieve when all is done. We have all lost parents in this, a strange way to form a bond I must say." She shrugged. "But the Fates do work in strange ways."

She shook her head, her expression changing, the veil of sadness lifting.

"Let's break our fast and talk about other things." The wind howled against the glass, lightning lighting the room. "If that's possible."

"Where is Ren this morn?" Xali asked as they followed her down the hall. She wanted desperately to talk to him about the dream.

"He is claiming the last of his Council. With Keary and…and my father leaving, the last places need to be filled. The new Council were called by the Fates early this morn."

"New Council?"

"There are always ten Lightbearers and ten Darkbearers. When one returns to the Fates, a new one is called. Usually that happens when a new king is about to ascend. Most of the Councils had returned to the Fates, training their replacements before leaving. Keary and my father knew they wanted to depart with Violissa and Sinow, so they waited. My father's replacement was called when another stepped down. I suppose the Fates knew Keepers needed to train their own. But that still left an opening when Father left. There must always be ten of each. The other Council have all been on for a few years, Cody and Eoin who were the youngest of Violissa's and Sinow's Councils remained and are now the elders."

She said it so nonchalantly that it must have been common knowledge, Xali and Carnick the outsiders still struggling to make sense of the ways of the immortals. She noted how Paige's voice had wavered when she'd mentioned her father, and Xali's own pain threatened to escape before she shoved it back to the recesses of her mind.

They broke their fast in a large dining room, the table the size of the one in the room they'd been in when Carnick and Ren had rescued her. The room was a blend of colors that calmed the soul, the walls a shade of green the hue of faded flower stems, light imprints of colored flowers flowing throughout. They were even in the gems that dangled around the candles that were alight with flames of sage. The ceiling, like the other rooms, too high to make out the soft imprints that adorned it. Floor-to-ceiling windows lined the outer wall looking out at a lush garden that spread into the forests far beyond. It was hard for Xali to see the true beauty of it with the violent storm still battering them. Thick gray hangings were pulled back from each window, a soft gray that brought out the etchings in the walls and added just enough touch of Dark to remind her that more than one power ruled this space.

Xali pushed her food around, barely touching it as Paige chattered on until, with a suddenness Ren burst through the doors, breaking the quiet calm that had settled upon them. His eyes were a deep onyx, and for a moment, Xali mistook him for his father until the blue trickled back in, his eyes settling on his wife.

"It is done," he said, reaching her and placing a kiss on her head. He sat next to her, the deep gray cape that had flourished behind him disappearing, his demeanor returning to the one Xali had come to know. He looked exhausted, and Xali wondered if he had slept at all.

Paige took his hand. "Glad to see you're back," she said, reaching up to the corner of his eyes as the final hint of black faded.

"Claiming a Dark Council, Paige. It's necessary."

"I know, I just miss the blue."

He kissed her hand then turned to Xali and Carnick.

"Looks like you've had a busy morn," Carnick said. "I miss productive morns."

Xali glanced at him, knowing he missed the simplicity of their former life, the consistency of it, the known that it had held.

"Would you take it back if offered?" Ren asked.

Carnick's eyes deepened, the storm clouds stirring. "No, never."

Xali smiled as his hand tucked back a strand of hair that touched her cheek.

"Then do not dwell on what no longer is. None of us has that luxury," Ren said, a sadness in his tone. Xali knew his parents were on his mind.

"They're really gone?" she said quietly.

A silence fell upon them, and she could see the magic fighting for dominance in Ren's aura. Did the Darkness shield his heart? She wished she had it to protect her own, to keep the rawness of her loss at bay. His cerulean eyes grew a rich blue that lie on the edge of black, his power a dichotomy to the hurting man below.

"Aye, we have all suffered losses, the future now handed to the four of us."

"The two of you," Carnick said. "I believe Paige and I are witnesses to what is coming."

"That we are, Carnick, but that doesn't lessen our part in all of it."

"She's right, Carnick," Ren said. "Paige was instrumental in saving my parents and helping my mother break free of my uncle's curse."

"Only because I had you by my side."

"I have no doubt you would have succeeded without me there. You are quite persistent. In fact, you did do it on your own the first time around."

She giggled, and for a moment, the blanket of sadness lifted, and they were as four friends eating together. Friends? A forced friendship, one sewn by her ancestor's misdeeds and the direction of the Fates.

Ren turned serious, and she wondered if her thoughts had been heard aloud. "You dreamed."

It wasn't a question; it was an absolute statement.

"Yes, I saw you, digging, searching, I saw the light over you before…before I saw it."

"You saw the Fate?"

She shuddered, the image creeping back, one that would haunt her forever.

"No, you didn't, did you?" he said.

"No." Her voice wavered.

"What did you see, Xali?"

She stayed silent, afraid speaking about it would make it real. But they were real, weren't they? The thing that had towered over her, terrifying in every aspect was a real god, one that was waking to wreak revenge on the Fates, regardless of the mortals who walked the land below them.

"Xali?" Carnick said, taking her hand.

"I saw…" She swallowed, her breath sticking in her chest, a flood of fearful tears rushing to her eyes.

"What did you see?" Ren demanded.

A stillness settled on the air, the flicker of the candles static as she said, "The old gods."

Thunder roared, the room shaking, the windows all shattering before the fragments froze midair, shards of glass aimed at them, drops of rain the size of stones hanging among them. Ren's eyes shone a vibrant violet.

Xali looked around, noting that Paige was frozen as well.

"You can freeze time?" Carnick answered.

"Around all but royal blood."

Lightning streaked across the sky, the clouds moving above, the ground rumbling. "And the Fates."

He moved his hand, and the glass fell along with the raindrops.

"You froze time?" Paige asked, moving once again and smacking his arm. "You promised not to do that!"

His violet eyes morphed to blue before they changed to black.

"Tell me about them," he said, moving his hand to re-form the windows, his eyes never leaving Xali's.

"If I do…it might make them real," she said quietly, a shiver running through her, Paige having the same reaction.

"They are real, and they're coming. We both saw the effects, the land ravaged—"

"The screams," she finished, the sound echoing through her mind.

"Screams?" Paige repeated, her voice low. "Fates, what did you two dream?"

"A nightmare," Ren answered for her.

The word nightmare hung in the air, Xali's fear polluting her aura, hanging around them all. Carnick had known she'd dreamed, her body tossing and turning as he'd watched helplessly until she'd woken in a frenzy. Chasing her down the halls that night, he'd had no idea what they were facing. Now it appeared there was far more left unsaid, forgotten in the chaos of Ren's family exiting the physical world.

Wrapping his arms around Xali, he pulled her close, feeling the tremors below.

"Why don't you start, Ren, since it seems you fared better in the dream," he said, wanting only to ease the burden for Xali, to take away the fear.

Ren ran his hands through his hair, his black eyes lighting to a shade closer to his normal color. He told his tale, Xali's shivering calming only slightly. The words he spoke did nothing to ease Carnick's state of mind; in fact, it only served to intensify his concern. He pictured the broken world, heard the screams of terror that had filled the dreams. The Fates had fallen, the war lost save a few left fighting. Was it an omen?

"Then she spoke to me, the Mother Fate. She said it was time. Time to take the crown, to let my parents go, that they were needed. That this was the only way to win the fight." He paused, hesitating to finish. "Then she was gone."

Silence followed until finally Carnick broke it.

"Do you often dream such foreboding omens?"

Ren's dark eyes met his. "I don't dream. Immortals rarely do."

"It wasn't an omen," Xali stated.

"Violissa's dreams were always warnings, foretellings," Paige said.

Carnick's heart pounded. "Always?"

Both Paige and Ren nodded.

"Xali, you didn't see or hear the Fate?"

"I saw her for a moment but only her light. Somehow, I knew it was her, but no, I didn't hear her. I was facing something…something darker. A god, the most terrifying thing I've ever seen. It sucked the life, the light from everything, shadowing it." She was whispering as if fearful her words might bring it to life.

They stared at her, no one knowing what to say. Carnick felt the quake of her body as he tucked his own fear away, knowing he needed to remain strong for her. He caught the shiver that went through Paige who was rubbing her arms in an attempt to rub away the image of what Xali had described. The stark contrast of the god to the Mother Fate was not lost to him, the light to the dark, the good to the horror of what the gods offered. His gods, those he and his family had worshipped. Those he had been trained to pray to since the earliest he could remember, to seek comfort in, to pay homage to, to know as the only deities.

Were they monsters? Truly? His mind couldn't envision how that could be so. He only knew them as the gods he'd worshipped at the shrine: understanding, benevolent, blessing his family with gifts that allowed them to rule his people…and to punish the other races. To demand obedience, to worship only their gods, or face death. Perhaps, they were monsters, his family shaped to become monsters in their own right. Rubbing his temples, he refocused on Xali and Ren.

"How did you know about my parents, Xali?" Ren asked, thankfully moving past the vision of the god.

"The land changed, it sprung to life, the god disappearing. There was a stream of colors, that of the magic your parents and you hold. With the rebirth of the land and those hues, I knew it had to mean they were meant to fight the battle. That without them, what I had seen would come to pass."

"All is not lost," Ren said. "That's what she said to me."

"The Mother Fate said that?" Paige asked.

"Yes. The Fates have hope. It lies in my parents and in us. You didn't hear anything she said? Not even that, Xali?"

"No, I was a bit preoccupied with the overbearing god towering over me."

"He took her," Ren said, a vacant look to his eyes.

"What?" Carnick asked. The more he heard, the more he wished he'd lingered in bed.

"The god took the Mother Fate…tearing her apart."

No one spoke, the impact of his words devastating. Paige looked a shade paler, and Xali's hand was frozen with fear, the fork she still held hovering above the plate. It slipped from her hand, the clink of its fall waking them all.

"What does it mean?" Carnick asked. "Are we to die, our world turned to the wasteland you described? The Fates and all of us lost?"

"No, it means there is hope," Ren answered.

"Hope? You just said that the Fates were dying. That the god Xali saw killed the Mother Fate. How can that give us hope?"

"I know I did!" Ren rose, his anger draping the room, eyes turning black with his apparent frustration.

"Ren," Paige said softly, and his power receded, his eyes softening.

"The Fates can win this battle, defeat the oncoming enemy, but they need help," Xali said as Ren continued to calm. "They can't win on their own. That's what she was showing us both. She came to you, Ren, because you are their child, your parents close enough to her heart to bring them into their fold. You were told by the Mother Fate of the potential of their ascension to the seat of the Fates, shown the reality of what would come to pass if that did not happen. You needed to be shown in order to help you move forward. I was shown the horror of what my family brought into this world and the potential of what your family will do to save it."

Her words made sense, but Carnick knew there was more to it than that.

"No, what all of you will do, Xali," he said. "You're as much a part of the solution as Ren and his parents." He sat back in his seat, running his hands over his face in an attempt to wipe away the seriousness of what they faced.

"He's right. My parents…the prophecy…all of it led to last night. Everything they went through, the tests they faced, all of it to prepare them for this moment."

"What?" Paige looked shocked.

"My parents are the embodiment of the Fates, the most power-ful rulers ever, my uncle almost equal in power to my father. The three have been claimed by the Fates, they were claimed long ago, before they were even born."

"By prophecy, yes," Paige said.

"By more than prophecy. My mother always said the Fates had their reasons, that the moves in the prophecy were all orchestrated, even Tynan's part."

"You mean the Fates knew this would happen?" Carnick asked, his mind still catching up.

"Not all of them," Xali said distantly. "But maybe some did. If we're part of this, Carnick, if I'm truly here for a reason, then maybe it's all part of what's to come, part of whatever prophecy is defining our moves."

"The Mother Fate knew. She knew the gods had been here first, that the actions of the other Fates at the beginning of this world would be their downfall."

"Then she also knew I would bring about that downfall."

They all stared at her, her words sinking into Carnick's heart.

"That's why the god revealed itself to me and the Fate to you. We are both tied to this in different ways. Without my actions, the gods would still be dormant."

"You can't know that, Xali," Carnick said.

"No? Our crazy aunt woke them somehow. I am the one who killed our uncle. The reason she lost her mind."

"No, my uncle killed your uncle with good reason," Ren argued.

"Maybe so but it is I who found you, set forth to wake all of you, including your uncle, thus unsettling the world, the balance within our family, I was the impetus."

Ren ran his hands through his hair and began to pace.

"Now what do we do?" Carnick asked.

"We fight," Xali said. "His parents were called to fight beside the Fates, as the last hope where we cannot reach. We have been called to fight down here where they won't be able to reach."

Pride rose within Carnick. She was a warrior at heart, a natural leader, and he would gladly fight to the death beside her.

"We find the remainder of your family first. Find out how your aunts did this and if there's a way to reverse it," Ren said, stopping his pacing.

"Can you sense them, Ren?" Paige asked. "Your father couldn't."

He shook his head. "It's as if they've faded from existence, their aura somehow hidden."

"Or something's shadowing it," Carnick said.

The windows rattled, the room creaking as the wind howled, the rain never ceasing.

"Whatever they've done to wake the gods, they're being shrouded, although I don't particularly think that bodes well for them," Ren said.

"So, we wait for a war to begin?" Paige asked.

"Yes, and in the meantime, we ready ourselves and our people."

"If this storm continues, the people will be hurting, the towns flooded. We can't even do anything in this weather."

"Then we'd best pray the storm lets up soon," Ren said.

"I don't think you want to see what this storm is bringing," Xali responded. "For when it stops, the war begins."

Fourteen

The storm continued for five more days. In that time, they prepared. Xali and Carnick called what troops were loyal to them.
Their dead were grieved, although the pyres could not be lit under
the soaking rain. There was little time for the grief to be claimed,
and so Carnick and Xali locked it away to be dealt with once the
battle ended. If it ever ended. Their family stayed away, all brought
to Xali's palace while Xali and Carnick remained in the northern
castle of the immortals, Ren's new home now that his parents were
gone. There was no time to talk to them, no time to evaluate what
loyalty remained. It would all be dealt with in the future once the
storm ended, once the war began.

It had yet to start, the anticipation making Carnick anxious.
With each passing day, his anxiety grew along with something else
that simmered just below the surface, stirred by small things, like

an ember below the quiet fire. He tried to ignore it, hoping it was simply the tense situation, the wait for the inevitable, but something about the feeling worried him. He kept it to himself, not wanting to add further concern to anyone's shoulders. The burdens were already too great.

Ren stayed silent, he and Paige grieving privately for their family. Carnick admired his stoic nature, feeling he'd lost his own, Xali's crowning having diminished it. He'd never pondered it before, the fact that his destiny had been cast aside for hers, his power second now, his status second. He would not rule as king with her at his side but the opposite. It was she who would make the decisions, lead her people, not his, not theirs. There was no longer a need for him to play that role or any role for that matter except that of her husband. A tinge of regret stirred along with that deeper sensation as he stood watching the storm. It was a feeling he hadn't had before, one he'd never had, and he wondered at its presence.

The feel of Xali's arms around his waist brought him back from whatever depth he'd sunk to, the thoughts disappearing with her touch.

"Hey," she said, kissing his back. He twirled her around so that she stood in his arms, all traces of his prior mood lost.

"Hey yourself," he said, kissing her.

She rested her head against his chest, and he held her there, relishing in the feel of her skin against his, the heartbeat that softly pounded in rhythm with his. They stood quietly watching as the storm drew on, wreaking havoc on the land below.

"When will it end?" Xali asked, and he wondered if she were referring to the storm or the myriad of events that had challenged their every step to happiness.

Kissing the top of her head, he whispered. "I don't have that answer." *I don't have any answers,* he thought.

The world was falling apart around them, and no one knew the next move. It was as if the world were flooding away. Ren's Councils were protecting the people, using their magic to move them to better shelter, to fortify their existing dwellings, but still, villages were being washed away.

A wicked crack broke the silence, echoing through the air and causing Xali to jump. Holding her tighter, Carnick scanned the world beyond the window, looking for any indication of what had been the cause. The room shook, along with the ground below, and an enormous cloud of dirt and smoke careened toward them, coating the castle.

Carnick held his breath, hearing Xali whisper, "They're here."

Tension sat upon him as he waited, watching fine spiderweb-like cracks form in the window before them. Entranced, he followed their pattern until the window was coated.

"Carnick," Xali said hurriedly, pulling at his arm. "Carnick, we need to move now!"

The window exploded toward them, but the fragments scattered to dust within the raging wind, his power transforming them. Xali's head was against his chest, and he could sense her fear in the shake of her body, smell it in the air. Never loosening his hold on her, he braced himself as the debris of dust and storm filled the room. His eyes focused beyond to where the rain had ceased, and blood-red covered the sky. They were here, and something about the fury of the now abated storm, the color of anger that layered the sky, the black that billowed from the mountains in the distance called to him.

It was an instinctual call, far within him, tainted and withered, an old magic.

As the dust settled, the room now coated, the world outside fell silent, a disturbing silence that caused the senses to scream in anticipation.

"Carnick." He heard. "Carnick, wake up, you're hurting me. Carnick!"

Wet vines wrapped around his arms and legs, wrenching him from Xali and from his state. Xali was pressed against the now empty window frame catching her breath, her eyes sparkling with emerald flecks that lie among the rolling storm clouds. He shrugged the vines from his skin, only their wet shiny residue remaining as they fell.

He looked to his hands then back to Xali who was now rubbing her arms.

"Gods, Xali, I'm sorry." He rushed to her, noticing the flinch as he pulled her to him. "I would never hurt you, I'm so sorry."

She looked up at him. "What happened, Carnick? Where did you go?"

"I, I don't know, the pull, there was something…I didn't know I was hurting you."

"What pull?"

"You didn't feel it?"

She shook her head, fear crossing her face. One of Ren's men appeared, causing Xali to jump. "Quite a mess in here," he said, his blue eyes studying them as though knowing he'd interrupted something he shouldn't have. "Ren asked that I check on you. He wants to see you both." His eyes turned toward the red sky. "Something is coming."

He shifted, leaving them where they'd been, awkwardly looking across from each other, a strange distance stepping between them. They remained there until Carnick finally pulled himself together and moved, stretching his hand out to lead her away from the window.

Tentatively, she accepted it as a coldness crept into his chest, one he didn't like.

"Come," he said, brushing a smudge of sand from her cheek. "We should get dressed and see what they know."

He turned away, but she grasped his hand.

"What was that, Carnick?"

He softened, bringing her hand to his lips.

"Nothing. I'm sure it's nothing more than my magic reacting to whatever has happened out there."

She stepped closer, pulling her hand free and running it along his cheek, letting it linger next to his eyes. "The flecks…your violet flecks, they shone red when the sky changed."

He took a step back, confused by her words.

"That can't be, they've only ever grown black. You must have seen wrong or maybe it was a reflection?"

"Did mine hold the same reflection?"

He shook his head, her words concerning him.

"I'm sure it was nothing," he said, unsure if he was trying to convince himself or her. "We should go before Ren sends another of his men in to startle you."

A glimpse of a smile appeared, and he pushed aside her words as well as the strange feeling he'd had earlier, knowing they needed to focus on the impending doom that shadowed their world, and hoping his feeling wasn't a foreshadowing of what was to come.

Ren was waiting for them in the meeting room they'd previously been in, only now Carnick noted the missing seats at the table. The new king, the only one who required a seat, with his Councils. Flames lit the fireplace, sending shadows upon the dark walls, one lone light sphere floating in the room, too dim to touch the black of the king's eyes. Carnick wondered at the color, why it now dominated the earlier blue that matched his Lightbearers.

"The storm has quieted, but the true torrent is surfacing. The mountain ranges in northern Tenebron have fallen, collapsed to nothing more than rubble," he said, the black fading to a rich sage. It was a strange transition, and Carnick had yet to grow accustomed to it.

Carnick knew the mountain ranges well. Northern Tenebron had fallen in his mother's province. He'd spent years memorizing the terrain in the province, preparing for the throne. The mountains had been part of that time, a place to which he'd always been drawn. They were majestic and striking, giving a feel of something ancient and powerful. They commanded attention, towering above the rest of the land, spreading from the edge of his uncle's province deep into his own until they grew to formidable heights in the Northwestern corner of their kingdom.

What was their connection to the inevitable war? To the gods? Why had they collapsed?

Too many questions collected in his mind, and he rolled his neck, that subtle fire within that he was still trying to ignore nipping at them with angst, uncomfortable with the unknown.

"And the gods?" Carnick asked, pushing the feeling away along with the abundance of questions.

Ren shook his head. "No sign of them yet, but I suspect they will show themselves soon. Fates help us when they do."

"They have your parents now, your uncle. The outcome of our dream has now changed," Xali said.

"Have you seen something?" Ren asked, the sage morphing to blue. Carnick wondered again at the transformations. It gave the appearance that he was having trouble controlling the blend of powers, each fighting for dominance within him. The thought didn't bode well if they indeed expected a ground war.

"No, just a feeling. They were called early in order to fight, weren't they?"

He sighed. "I believe so. The dream we had was a foreshadowing of what was to come, but I believe you were right, it was meant for me to understand why they were being called early, why my ascension would not come in the same way as every other king's ascension has. It was all leading up to this war we're awaiting. My parents have always carried power that verged on those of the Fates. My uncle always predicting they had a higher calling, and he was correct."

He had suggested something similar the morning after they'd been called, and Carnick still wasn't certain he understood. Were his Fates that aware of future events? Their lives so predictable that free will was obsolete among the immortals?

"You sound as though the Fates knew this would happen," he said.

"Nothing in this world happens without reason. Perhaps not all the Fates foresaw this, but the Mother Fate certainly did as likely the other Fates who created my parents' prophecy."

"All of it leading to this?"

"I don't truly know. Whatever the reason, we are all part of it and must see it out to the end. The Fates now have their army. And we have ours." Ren ran his hands through his hair.

"So, what do we do now?" Carnick asked, tired of waiting for the inevitable.

"Your people are being evacuated, those who are able will be placed in your palace, and those beyond its capacity will be moved to our safeholds in the castles."

"But we all agreed they would be safe, that our aunts would never harm their own people."

"This is bigger than what your traitorous aunts could have imagined when they unleashed the gods. Your lands are closest to the mountains, and they will be the first to fall if these things are anything like our dream leads them to be. There will be no distinction, they will see all of the Fates' children as their enemy."

"But we've never seen ourselves as the Fates' children. We've always worshipped the gods," Carnick argued.

"And did your gods ever look like Xali described?" Ren's voice held an edge to it, his eyes growing deeper in shade.

"No, but the façade we worshipped looked unlike the Fates as well." Carnick couldn't help the sneer that accompanied his reply. As Ren's power seemed to vacillate, so his own was flickering on the edge of release.

"He has a point, Ren," one of the men said. "We cannot guarantee that we will have the time nor the capacity to move all of their people. If he's right, then they stand to be in no danger."

"And you would take that chance, Uncle?"

Carnick and Xali both looked at the man, his auburn hair messy against his intense blue eyes. He looked nothing like Ren, and it was the first they'd heard of a second uncle.

"I would argue that our resources are needed elsewhere."

Ren's eyes darkened to the cusp of ebony.

"He's right, Ren, their people are not our concern. If those beasts are coming, we need to preserve our strength."

Ren flicked his head to the black-haired man, power sweeping through the room like a thick cloak.

"All of the people in these lands are my people to protect, regardless of their origins or their past."

No one else spoke, and a strange silence followed, Ren's attention turning back to the one he'd called uncle, the man distinctly dressed in white with the eyes of someone with Light magic.

After a few moments, the air simmered, Ren's demeanor shifting, the room calming. He swiped his hands through his hair.

"The Lightbearers will see to the evacuation of who they can. Darkbearers, I want you preparing. Whatever is coming will reveal itself soon. Cody, Eoin, Thane, you will accompany Xali and Carnick to their palace."

"No, you need us here," Xali argued.

"Not yet I don't. You are queen, you need to be seen by your people who do not understand why the world has erupted into chaos, why they are being moved once again. You need to see those remaining family who are loyal to you, assign figureheads to lead the people while you fight. And you need to select fighters to stand with us against the coming onslaught."

"We've called our armies," Carnick said.

"They will be of minimal help. We need magic, and your family has it, even if it has diminished. It will still help. They need to fight by your side just as you will fight by mine."

"Eoin, Thane, you are to guard these two. I don't care what happens to anyone else. They are the priority. Cody will accompany as healer in case you two fail."

"We will not fail."

"I know. If you do, you know the punishment that awaits you." The ebony took over, dominating the other colors within Ren's eyes; the Dark king was present and in control.

The two men nodded with a slight bow then walked toward Xali and Carnick.

"I suppose guard duty is my punishment, Ren?" the one named Cody said.

"You are the only one I trust to ensure they stay alive, Uncle," he returned. "I will call you when the time draws close."

Before they could protest, the room disappeared, and Carnick found himself in the front garden of the palace, or what had been the front garden at one time. Debris littered the place, rubble spewed in every direction from the stone walls that no longer stood on the outside of the palace. Trees were downed and strewn everywhere, glass littered the stairs leading into the building. A mist of ash fell upon them, the effect as if a fresh snow had covered the ruined state of their home.

"This is why he wants your people protected," one of them said.

An eerie silence surrounded them, an unnatural one, and Xali moved closer to Carnick, the chill that went through her evident as she drew near.

"Let's get you inside." The two who now wore black capes, pulled their hoods up and walked, ushering them forward.

The other, the uncle, did not draw his hood.

"You're Ren's uncle?" Xali asked, her curiosity always too piqued to stay quiet, something Carnick usually found adorable, but today, it grated on him. They needed to be inside, away from the destruction, from the strange feel to the air, the thickness that sent his senses tingling, the pull far below straining. He rolled his neck, trying to clear it from his consciousness as he listened to the answer.

"I'm Violissa's brother. It's a long story, and Sinow argues to this day that I'm not." He laughed then the smile faded. "Argued."

"Another of those stories from the past I'm hoping to hear one day when all of this is over?"

"Exactly. Now let's catch up before these two get irritated.

Darkbearers are not known for their patience."

Mendol greeted them when they entered the palace. Xali ran to him, throwing her arms around him, having missed her brother terribly. She watched as Carnick shook his hand then embraced him. Fairenth came loping down the corridor, tripping on her gown as she entered the open foyer, Carnick helping her up and sweeping her into a hug. She looked small, fragile in the midst of the destruction that lie around them. Her eyes were bloodshot like she'd spent every night crying, her normally fashioned hair, loose and knotted.

"The others are awaiting your arrival. One of the king's men informed us that you would be arriving."

Xali ruffled his hair; she'd missed him more than she'd thought possible, remembering how she'd worried for him when she'd been held prisoner, worried that they wouldn't live to see each other again.

He nodded to Cody, a familiarity to the look.

"Good to see you fully recovered, Mendol."

"Thanks to your steady hands."

"You healed him?" Xali asked.

"Aye, he was put in my care."

She smiled, tears brimming the corners of her eyes. "Thank you."

"Eh, all part of the job. He did put up quite a fight though."

There was a gleam in his eye, a bit of humor, and she wondered what he was like outside of his expected duties.

As they came upon the great hall, Xali took in the familiar sight of her family, her heart lurching at the absences. Everyone stayed silent, the heavy gloom in the air palpable. They had lost more than their fair share, and Xali was the reason for their losses. Nothing could erase that fact, no matter how one decorated it with magic and crowns. Xali was the only one who had fared well, even with the death of her father and the brutal imprisonment she'd endured factored in.

Finally, after what seemed an abyss of silence, her mother rose. She approached Xali and folded her in her arms. The action almost shattered Xali, almost tipping the dam that held her emotions, her tears at bay.

Her mother's move broke the trance, and soon, they were all greeting her and Carnick, although some greetings were tinged with resentment. It wasn't visible, but Xali could feel the tentativeness of the hugs, the stiffness. They were still wary of her, and she wondered if there were any who remained against her in the room. Could she ever trust any of them after what she'd gone through?

The room fell to a hush as Xali and Carnick went through the events, Xali shocking them all with the cruelty of her aunts and cousin.

"I knew she'd lost it," Trevant said. "She'd been talking to herself, turning nasty each day further from father's death. But I never thought she was capable of this. Nor did I think Sartria was."

Herind clasped his shoulder in support.

"You were naïve, Trevant. This is always what Sartria has been like," Carnick said.

Trevant eyed him; there was no doubt he knew Sartria's true desires, what she'd intended with Carnick. Xali knew, so it stood that Trevant knew. There had always been a part of her that wondered if Carnick had indulged their cousin's wants, had bedded her before her joining with Trevant. There would have been nothing stopping him; first borns were not under the same rules to remain chaste, although it was frowned upon to do so with others in the family. Sartria was tempting, she wouldn't have questioned it if Carnick had taken her, but it would have stung. She'd never asked, preferring to stay ignorant and believing that he would never have done such a thing to her.

"She wasn't faithful, but she was never a murderer, Carnick," he argued, his tone terse.

"I agree with Trevant," Xali said. "Sartria has always been… ambitious. And never has she hidden the fact that she envies me for our betrothal"—Xali glanced at her hands—"or disliked me for other reasons, but the person I saw that day…that wasn't our cousin. That was someone else."

Silence ensued, no one having any thoughts as to why Sartria had changed, why she'd sided with the others, other than ambition for a throne that had been stripped from her.

"So, you fled, all of you, seeking shelter outside the palace away from Sartria and the others?" Carnick asked, moving the focus from their cousin. "You must have realized she and the aunts had lost it."

"Not until it was too late. When she and Aunt Katama attacked your mother and Xali's father, we fled," Trevant said.

"You didn't stay to fight for them?" Xali asked, hurt that they'd run.

"We did until Mendol fell, and we knew our best chance was to get to you."

"To get to the immortals," Ainia added. "Our mothers both lost it, and Sartria went right along with them. All of them acting like their minds were no longer their own. That was not my mother. Trevant's right. Father's death did something to her, changed her. I'd expected her to mourn as we did, but she didn't. She grew hard, callous, her words no longer her own. Something had taken over her. She whispered to Aunt Katama. I would hear them."

"And over time, she changed my mother," Herind added. "Both of them mumbling about you, Xali, the treason you committed, how you needed to pay. When your father and Aunt Renia arrived, we were hopeful they could reason with them, return them to their former selves, but whatever it was that had turned them had already corrupted them."

"There was something invasive there," Fairenth said quietly. "It would slink in the shadows, I could feel it calling to my magic." She shuddered.

"I felt it, too."

"As did I," the agreements echoed around the room.

Xali rubbed her arms, unsure what to make of their words, of what her aunts had invited into that palace.

"How did Xali's father die?" Carnick asked.

"I don't want to know, Carnick," Xali whispered. "I had to watch as your mother took her last breath. I don't want to hear the rest."

"I know," he said, taking her hand, "but I have a suspicion it's important given what they just told us."

"Are you certain you want to know?" Ainia asked.

"Yes, we do."

Ainia sighed, but it was Mendol who spoke.

"After Father and Aunt Renia arrived, we didn't see them again for several days. When any of us inquired, we were told they were in deep talks with Aunt Katama. It didn't seem suspicious, they were the remaining three heads, it was ordinary business. But then, after several days, Sartria began acting strange, spending less time with us and disappearing. "

Mendol paused, looking down at his hands as if the memory were too hard to keep in place. After several seconds of silence, he looked back up at them and continued.

"We were summoned to the courtyard by Uncle Lengan, told to meet there and await news. We thought perhaps they'd come to an agreement, settled the differences, the anger over your crowning finally simmered. They dragged Father out to the courtyard. He and your mother, Carnick. Accused them both of treason. Neither could talk, they'd bound their mouths and hands. They were powerless somehow, both covered in bruises so that we could see they'd fought hard to avoid being restrained. I tried to stop the three of them, we all did, but we couldn't. They were too strong, their power had not diminished but strengthened. We were unable to even get close enough to interrupt what they were doing. I was throwing everything at Aunt Hastrial when out of nowhere Sartria attacked me."

"None of us could move to help," Fairenth said. "Mendol was situated apart from us, and Sartria was occupying him. Once the first drop of blood fell from Uncle, the skies darkened, and we were pushed back by some force. Unwilling witnesses to his death." A sob escaped her, the memory too fresh, and Xali held her own tears back.

"I was caught in the fight with Sartria," Mendol said. "I almost had her bested when she stabbed me. I don't know where the knife had been hidden, but she did enough damage that I could only watch helplessly with the others as Father bled out across the ground." He stared absently while the words hung in the air.

Tears rolled down Xali's face, no longer banished behind the dam that had now burst.

"They kept Mother alive," Fairenth said. "They stabbed her." Her voice broke. "Cut her in so many places that the blood was like a second skin. We couldn't do anything. Something held me, dark and hot, it had wrapped around my legs and my arms, it was invasive." The last word came out as a whisper.

"They didn't kill your mother there. They left her to die in the dungeons," Xali said.

"They didn't need her anymore," Carnick said absently. "They needed you, your blood to complete the ceremony."

Xali's eyes flew to him as the reaction was heard around the room.

"Don't you see? That's why they left you to die in that courtyard, Xali. They needed your blood. Your father was just the beginning, the initial sacrifice, my mother's blood needed to fortify whatever that sacrifice had been for."

"But she didn't die until the day they tried to kill me."

"One quick death to heed the call," Trevant said.

"What?"

"That's what Mother said when I confronted her before we escaped. I didn't know what she'd meant. I thought she'd finish Mendol off or take one of us."

"That's when you ran?"

"Yes, we grabbed Mendol and ran because we didn't agree with what they'd done. We were appalled, devastated."

"Scared they'd turn on us," Fairenth said. "Mother…she looked at me as she lay there. I could see the word in her eyes, that she wanted us to run, to flee to safety. She was so stubborn, even like that. She gave me that look like she would when she expected us to obey. So, I obeyed."

There was a moment of quiet, and Xali knew Carnick was thinking on his mother. They all knew the look of which Fairenth spoke, Aunt Renia the strictest of the elders. Where Crebant's power had been in the physical abuses of his family, Renia's had been in her steel gaze and in her words. Xali had seen it, been the receiver of it often, even as her aunt had lain in death her words had been like a brandished sword, cutting away at her resolve.

"Of course, you did. And they let you run, knowing that you would bring them what they really needed," Carnick said.

"Xali," Mendol said sadly. "I sent you right to them, they knew we'd seek you out."

"Knew she'd be foolish enough to come on her own, too emotional to wait for help."

"He was my father, Carnick."

"And she my mother!" he yelled, his eyes flickering to black. She took a step back as a shade of red replaced the violet specks that had once been there. "You shouldn't have gone, you should have gone to the immortals!"

"And none of this would be happening? That's what you want to say," she returned, hurt, stinging from his sudden turn.

"Carnick, she did what any of us would have done," Mendol said in her defense.

The air was thick with his power, a strange mix of Darkness and something else that gave Xali pause.

His eyes softened, the tension fleeing his muscles. "I'm sorry, Xali. I don't know where that came from."

Xali noticed Ren's Darkbearers had entered the room, standing at the edge of the doorway, their magic drawn. She didn't think they'd come here to protect her from her husband, but now they read him as a threat.

"Why would any of them need to die?" Fairenth asked, turning her attention from Carnick's unsettling outburst.

"Yes, what is it you haven't told us in your story?"

"They called the gods," Xali answered hesitantly.

"The gods? But I thought the Fates were our gods all this time?"

"They were. The Fates created us, they were our true gods, but the immortals think there may have been other gods on this world before it became the Fates'. Gods long ago defeated, buried."

"And you think our mothers woke these sleeping gods?" Trevant asked.

"The same gods we've been worshipping since our people turned their back on the Fates," Carnick said.

Silence fell, not even a breath was heard.

"But our gods are gentle, protective," Fairenth said.

"Gods for whom our people have been shedding blood of non-believers for millennia," Xali said, the thought terrifying her. "We've been sacrificing to them since we stepped foot on this land. And now they've been awakened."

"By horrible, vindictive servants who are handing them vengeance," Carnick added.

"What do you need from us?" Xali's mother asked. She'd been silent, along with Carnick's father as they'd talked. Xali was surprised to hear her speak so confidently, knowing she was still in mourning. "Our family created this mess. What is needed to undo it?"

"I think this mess was created long before any of the races were here, our family simply fueling it," Carnick said. His voice was distant, and Xali wondered what was going through his mind. Likely the same terror that was flooding hers, but there was something still off about him, something not quite right.

"Xali," her mother said, bringing her focus back.

"We need your power. What magic is left in what remains of us. It is thought that two battles will be waged. One on ground and one between the gods and the Fates. With the return of their king and queen to fight on the Fates' side, we are down two immortals on our own side."

"Three," Carnick corrected. "We lost the brother as well."

"Lost them?" Trevant asked.

"Yes, Ren has ascended to the throne and the others taken to stand beside the Fates."

"I thought they were immortal? They're gone?"

"It's part of their ascension, the prior king returns his soul to the Fates. Only this time, the Fates took the three of them, making them one of their own, adding to their own army."

"Gods, Xali"—Mendol sounded defeated—"the Fates took them? So, we're left with one immortal? They're side is strengthened, and we're left with one immortal?"

He had a point, but something she remembered Ren's uncle saying led her to believe that having Ren as a lone immortal alongside his Council was all they needed.

"Ren is strong, and he has his Councils, so he's not simply one immortal."

"But we're not immortal, and our magic has already begun to wane from the curse the Fates befell us."

"And why should we fight for them when they're taking our magic, our land, our titles, everything from us?" Ainia asked.

Carnick tensed, and the Darkbearers moved closer.

"It's a valid question," Mendol said, "and I'm sure not one that was ill-intended."

Carnick evaluated his cousin, looking for any threat, but it was Xali who answered, knowing Carnick was on edge.

"I know not all of you are happy with what's happened, that some of you blame me for all of it, even what's happening now, but I, like you, am simply a pawn in something greater than titles and land. What happens in the course of these next few days, even moons, will define the fate of our world whether it continues to exist or is wiped away like dust on a table. We have the power to fight, to show our people that we are still united, still their royal family regardless of who holds the true title."

She felt Carnick's eyes on her but remained focused on the cousins. They were quiet, glancing at each other, small nods given to one another until Herind said, "We will fight with you, little cousin."

Relief swept through her, the tension fleeing her muscles.

"Good," Carnick said, but Xali noticed his tension had not faded.

"So, what now?" Carnick's father asked.

It was then that Xali realized all but one first born head remained, one dying at the hands of the immortals, the other two at the hands of the remaining first born, her aunt. Perhaps it wasn't Crebant whose need for vengeance had destroyed their houses. Perhaps it was truly Katama whose need for power had threatened their very existence.

"Yes, Xali," Carnick's father said softly as if reading her thoughts. "Crebant was always a threat to our house and yours, but it was Katama who pulled the strings. My sister is manipulative and power hungry."

"She's driving Hastrial, isn't she? Fueling her anger at Uncle Crebant's death and playing on her emotions."

"I have no doubt. She will fight you for your crown any way she can, for it is the crown she wants, the one that rules all the houses. She will bring anyone down who stands in her way. She would have turned on Crebant the minute he defeated your father's house and ours."

"She already has," Xali said with a sigh, wondering how she'd failed to see the devious sides of her family, the undercurrent of jealousy and treason that shrouded it.

"You were too far removed from it, Xali, lost in your own world, finding your own way. The rest of us saw it," Mendol said. "Not to the extent that it played out, but we were well aware of it."

She turned to Carnick. "You as well?"

He nodded. "Mother taught me early to trust no one, to always be wary, kin or no kin. The crown, power it corrupts even the strongest, and both Katama and Crebant were seen as the weaker of the two heads."

"They wanted what your father and Renia had. Even as children. When you were born, Crebant saw you as a threat, only dismissing you when your magic failed to develop. I have no doubt he would have found a way to kill you if it had flourished then. He knew what the full emerald moons meant, that they did not spell out a bad omen but a sign of power."

"A sign of power?" she asked.

"Yes." Her mother looked to Carnick's father.

"Go ahead, there is no need for further secrets," he told her.

"There was a writing found behind the guardian wall—"

"The Elvin Enclave," Carnick corrected.

"Yes. The great king tried to destroy it but to no end. It was bewitched with magic greater than his. So, he buried it far below the land, hiding it so no one would ever discover it."

"But someone did?" Carnick asked.

"No," his father answered. "It has never been seen. The great king told his sons about it on his death bed. Ramblings of a dying man, but they held onto the story, wary of its meaning."

Xali's curiosity was piqued.

"It told of the emerald moons, that they would reveal the turn of power of our people, the child who would restore what was lost, free us from the curses of our forefathers."

"No, Pibron, the curses of our makers," her mother corrected Carnick's father.

"Yes, thank you, that was it."

Xali stood, mouth agape, unable to fathom why she'd never heard of this, why the knowledge had been hidden from her.

"A prophecy," Cody said from behind her.

The room was silent. Xali's head was spinning, and she grabbed Carnick's arm.

"Why did none of us know this?" Carnick asked, steadying her.

"It is part of the crowning, the secrets are given upon your oath to the crown. Your betrothed would have been sworn to the same oath."

"There was a prophecy about me," Xali said.

"One that ties in with Ren's," Cody said from behind them. "One that if heeded rather than shunned may have prevented all of this."

"Perhaps not, Cody," one of the Darkbearers said. "The Fates are fickle. There must always be a means to whatever the end is."

"The gods. The end is the war with the gods. The curse I'm to free us from is the one the Fates brought about."

"Maybe not, Xali. What if it was the stealing of the land, the severing of the kingdom from the immortals?"

"No, the kingdom was already a cursed one before we stepped foot on it. Something bigger is playing out, a wound that has been festering since before even the immortals and their people were created."

"And how do we stop it, how do we stop a war and break whatever the curse is?"

"We don't. I do," she said. "I've already made the first steps, created the catalyst for the events that will unfold. It's up to me... and Ren to right the wrongs, to fix this."

"And what happens to you in all of this?" Carnick asked, taking her hand.

"I don't know," she whispered, fear rippling through her with the words. This was far bigger than any of them had imagined, and it had been written in prophecy, one that tied to the greatest prophecy their world had known. One that tied her to Ren and his fate, the two now intersected on a course with an ending that spelled the end of all they knew.

Fifteen

The sound of his footfalls beat a steady rhythm, but Ren ignored it, continuing instead to pace the study. Two days had passed since the world had stilled, and nothing but an unnatural silence had followed. He stopped, his fingers running the span of the desk beside him. Looking down, he took in the worn patches, the signs of the men who had sat before him, of his father whose study it had last been.

He touched the wood as if it might bring his father back, his presence sorely missed. How he wished he were here to guide him. Wished his mother's gentle smile were upon him, her calming magic steadying the storm of magic within him. The thoughts that would not quiet.

Lifting his fingers, he backed away from the desk, knowing he was lingering in the past, in desires he could not attain. He was on his own in this, the Fates deeming he was ready, no matter how unsure he felt about it.

He wasn't truly alone, though. Xali and Carnick were on this journey with him. Cody had relayed the discovery of a lost piece of the prophecy, one that distinctly referenced Xali. One that connected her to everything that was happening as well as the final outcome. He moved his hands through his hair, frustrated that someone so innocent, so young, and with powers that were too new to her was meant to carry such a burden. And where did he fit in with this new revelation? Was it all tied to what he'd seen in the guardians' lair? Or a piece of the words he'd been unable to translate? He wished he had his father here to talk to, his uncle to guide his thoughts, his mother to calm his unsettled spirit.

Walking to the windows that ran from floor to ceiling, he pulled aside the window coverings to stare outside. The world had fallen silent, a stasis hanging over it like a foreboding fog. *Something is coming*, his instinct screamed. It had been screaming for days now, and try as he might, he could not quiet it.

He didn't feel prepared for whatever it was, gods or their minions, they weren't ready. His Council was too new, unweathered, unsteady still. Two were so new they wouldn't be able to fight, their power in its infancy, unsure of themselves and how to control it. Yet they would be forced to fight. He prayed the bones that had layered his dreams were not hiding the bones of his Council below.

Something nudged at his senses, stirring the Elvin in him. He sent his nature powers forth, spanning the distance of Tenebron. The land was stirring, filled with unrest, weary of something. As his power drew closer to the obliterated mountains, his Dark power tensed then rose to match the nature. The ground stirred, a rumble emitting from far below and with it a sensation that ripped through Ren's senses. He drew back but not fast enough, a grip tightening around his power, pulling him. He was forced to shift, whatever it was shifting him from the room.

He found himself in the rubble of the mountains. Fire spewed from below, the power still strangling his own. He didn't fight it, knowing he was meant to see. A crack filled the sky as lightning touched down around him. Heat soared through him, almost unbearable until the black skies opened up and a gentle cooling breeze touched his face.

Mother.

They were there, the Fates were watching just as he was. Witness to the return of what horrors had walked their lands before they had. The ground quivered at the assault. Movement caught his eye, and he saw Xali. She was stumbling back, looking around wildly.

"Damn," he muttered. Whatever force had summoned him here, it had pulled her as well. She was too much a part of whatever this was to not bear witness, but she was mortal, vulnerable.

He ran to her, the ground erupting with each step, juts of fire tearing from below, spewing lava and rock around him. He threw his Light magic at her, shielding her. He couldn't shift, whatever force had dragged him here didn't want him leaving. Across from Xali, two figures rose. Women garbed in black.

Her aunts. What in the Fates were they doing in the middle of this? They'd been undetected, hiding here all this time. They were staring at Xali whose attention was on the rift that had opened before her. She teetered on the edge, fire streaming on every side of her, his protection spell the only reason she remained unscathed.

Ren ran, the ground continuing to buckle as he threw her back with his magic. She tumbled and rolled, the ground lifting, a massive hand clawing through it.

Grabbing her, he moved them back. He looked to the aunts, tense and ready for their attack, but they remained in place, observers to the chaos they had birthed.

From the rift emerged terrifying creatures, winged beasts whose screeches cut the air with a deafening sound. Beasts on four legs that made even their largest wolves look like pups, deformed two-legged creatures that moved in fire, their skin as lava. The things tore from the ground and ran loose, Ren too stunned to move, Xali clinging to him, her body shaking with fear.

The hand that had clawed through the stone pulled its body out of the rift, standing to tower over them, more joining it. They resembled men but for their size and tar-like skin that looked to be made from the depths of the hottest volcano. It roared, and everything shook, the moons cracking, long ridges developing through them.

Ren's heart pounded. How were they ever to fight this?

You cannot fight them, Ren. Run, Ren. Take her far from here now! His father's voice echoed through his head. He tried to shift but whatever they'd done had left it locked. He pulled Xali and ran.

"What are you doing, Ren?"

"Following my father's orders."

He lost his footing, the ground opening before them. He threw Xali to the side then leaped to grasp the ridge, pulling himself up as debris rained down around them. He scrambled to Xali, and then they were both thrown backward, the gods now all above them, moving to reclaim their world.

"Look!" Xali yelled, pointing to the sky where the stars were dropping.

"The returned immortals," he said, hauling her up. The ones who'd chosen a life among the stars, given breath once again by the Fates to join the fight.

They landed with massive explosions around the devastated land. Ren felt his eardrums burst as Xali screamed in pain, her hands holding her ears, blood trickling from her nose. She was too fragile, this was no place for a mortal. He healed her and took her hand again as the fallen stars took shape.

"Why can't we shift?" Xali yelled.

"I don't know. They pulled me here, and I haven't been able to loosen that power from their grasp."

Men had appeared, dwarfed by the gods. The former Dark and Light kings and Councils from the past, his ancestors. They pummeled the gods with their magic. Within seconds, the land transformed into a war ground, but the gods undid everything the returned immortals threw at them. They were no match for them.

Ren, his mother's voice called. *You must run, this battle is ours, you have your own demons to fight.*

It was then that the sky turned a blinding white with golden and silver figures descending. Ren couldn't look away as the full force of the Fates rose before him, something no one had ever witnessed. The gods roared, debris lifting around them, the returned immortals all flung back as the eight larger-than-life gods faced the Fates.

"Ren, look!" Xali yelled against the noise, the battle ensuing, magic greater than any he knew filling the air like an electric current.

He needed to get her out of here, but his eyes looked to where she pointed. His breath stuck in his chest. His father was there, a glowing silver figure among the other Fates, fighting one of the gods, the power around him visible in a black haze that shimmered silver. His uncle fought beside him enshrouded in that same power.

In the distance, his mother stood beside the Mother Fate, her magic bright against the darkness that seemed to be settling around them. Together, they worked the land, healing it, shaping it to a weapon, lethal as it jutted below the gods, tearing at their armored skin.

A flash of black paired with a deafening crack threw the two women back. His father, his attention pulled to his mother momentarily was hit with a force that sent him flying, the ground collapsing below him, swallowing him. He soared from the gap, landing with a ground-quivering boom. His mother was in the fray now, battling the same god, his uncle beside her. Her father's anger spilled around him like a shroud.

"Ren, Ren, I think we can shift now," Xali said, grabbing at him.

She was right, something in him had loosened, the magic freeing, but as he called it, she was torn from his grasp. He tried reaching her as her scream ripped through the discord but was too late. Any other immortal would have shifted, but she was not immortal and remained untrained in so many aspects of her magic. He'd stopped their lessons, and so she was pulled away, a particularly brutal looking god lifting her with his power. Ren shifted to her proximity, calling his magic, but as he aimed it toward the god, it turned his eyes to Ren, Xali still struggling in its hold.

Ren froze, the power in those eyes ancient and immeasurable, red light tearing through the pitch-black orbs. The breath was pulled from his lungs, and no matter that he was the strongest of his line, he was powerless in that moment.

The invisible grip on him tightened, and he helplessly watched on. The god pinned Xali to the ground. Around them, the battle continued, none of the others noticing the situation as it studied Xali.

You are the bringer of destruction, chaos abounds within you. Its voice echoed through Ren's head but was directed at Xali.

Xali's two aunts were dragged toward the god and landed unceremoniously next to her.

Why should I kill one who feeds us?

"You promised!" the one aunt answered, the god's voice echoing through all their minds.

She was lifted in the air as it tipped its head at her then ripped her apart with its power, its gaze never wavering. Ren thought he would be sick, the Dark power in him rising to accept the viciousness of the attack, the punishment given but the Light appalled at the horror of it. Xali screamed while the other aunt scrambled away, no longer the god's concern.

It laughed as Xali struggled.

I think I'll kill the Fates' pet and save you for later. You are necessary but your death must be at the right time and by the right hand. Now is not that time. Now is the time for revenge. You, his eyes turned to Ren, *are dispensable, and your death will cause them pain. You die first.*

The grip tightened around Ren, the reality of his imminent death heavy upon him as he felt his immortality seeping away. He struggled as it flowed from him, weakness making its way through him, his powers coiled within a vice that would not allow them freedom. Then he heard it, a scream that shook the torn land below them, his mother's scream. Her powers flared, blinding in its force, and the grip released, the flow severed, his immortality plunging back to his cells, his core.

The god was thrown back, its grip on Xali loosened.

Take her, Ren, now! His father's voice boomed through his head.

Ren didn't hesitate. He shifted to Xali, pulling her to him and shifted away as the god fell with an ear-splitting blow brought down by his mother whose magic still lingered on his skin when they landed in the courtyard of the keep.

He kept a tight hold on Xali, his eyes drawn to the place where once the massive mountain range had stood. The land was no longer flattened, having risen high into the sky. Orbs of gold, silver, and black danced along the top. To any unknowing being, it would have been entrancing, save for the black cloak that enshrouded the land past it, and the flames that licked the clouds, clouds red as blood. Ren knew, however, that a battle was taking place, one that would determine the fate of them all.

Sixteen

Quakes of fear cascaded through Xali's body, and no matter how she tried, she couldn't stop them. The image of the god was etched in her mind as a deep scar that would never fade, as was the brutal murder of her aunt. The bile climbed its way to her mouth, and she vomited, the terror no longer holding it at bay.

Ren didn't move, his eyes still fixed on the flashing lights in the distance. She wiped her mouth with the back of her hand.

"Can you see them?" she managed.

"Yes, our vision is superior to that of mortals."

"But your power is no match for the gods." She hadn't meant for it to be any more than an honest statement and hoped he didn't take it that way.

"No, it's not." He gripped his hands tight, and she could see that the thought of being weak angered him.

He'd tried to help her, tried to get to her, but the god had stopped him, holding him in its grip just as it had her. She'd been standing at the window, watching the storm, unable to sleep and not wanting to wake Carnick. His own sleep had been restless recently, and it was good that he finally slept. She worried about him. There was something different about him, something just under the surface since the day the storms had started. She couldn't quite discern what it was, but it felt dark to her. The beautiful violet flecks of his eyes would succumb to a fiery red. It didn't last long, but it was there for just enough time for her to notice. He didn't seem aware of the change, but she was.

She'd watched him sleeping, his face contorting as a nightmare held him, then just as quickly, it had come, it released him, his breath calming, face peaceful again. Finally, she'd risen to gaze at the storm, feeling its intensity grow until something grabbed her, pulling her from her spot to the mountains, the world in chaos around her, the calm of her room gone. She'd been disoriented, stumbling to adjust to her surrounding, fear shredding her soul. How had she gotten there? Who or what had brought her?

Her attention had been pulled to the enormous rift that had opened before her, then Ren had been there, pulling her away, trying to save her.

She looked to him now, his usual confident stature seemingly diminished. He'd been to that god as any mortal would have been to him, his power useless. It had to have been a reality-shattering moment to him. He was weak against the gods, just as weak as she was. But they weren't meant to fight the gods. The image of the stars falling, of his parents, larger than life, glowing with the brilliance of the Fates upon their auras, came to her until a screech that sent chills down her spine broke the silence. The gods would be fought by their own kind, the Fates. The monsters they had unleashed, however, would be theirs to fight. The chill gripped her like a vise as she thought of the creatures she'd seen, things of nightmares.

"What do we do now, Ren?" she whispered, her voice quaking.

A howl split the night air. "We fight the beasts they unleashed and pray the battle goes in our favor."

"And to whom do we pray? The Fates or the gods?" He turned to her, the blue of his eyes now an endless onyx. She didn't wait for a response, saying in a whisper, "And will anyone even hear us?"

His eyes grew sad, the black morphing to a night blue. "I don't know," he said before turning back to the battle in the distance. "I truly don't know."

Carnick woke, suddenly disoriented until he remembered they'd returned to the northern castle that had been Ren's home as Ren still did not fully trust their family enough to leave Xali out of his protection. His sleep had been fraught with nightmares again, images of beasts like Xali had described from her own nightmare, thoughts that burrowed into his mind, feelings of unrest, and the need to hurt. They were the same each night, and as he sat up, rubbing the sleep from his eyes, he worried at his sanity. The endless invasion of Darkness that he felt from the dreams was wearing him down. But it wasn't truly Darkness, not like the power he'd come to recognize. This was different, that strange, foreign pull that he'd experienced the few times when he'd seemed lost to Xali.

It worried him, but he kept silent, unwilling to burden her with anything more than was already occurring. He'd deal with it after this mess of a war was over, if it ever started.

He stretched and only then realized that Xali was not sleeping next to him. Had he woken her with his stirring? He looked across the room to see her at the window. Her silhouette in the moonlight that shone through stirred his desire for her. With all that had happened, the exhaustion that seemed ever present, the worry that held them hostage, they'd barely had time for intimacy. Silently, he cursed the Fates for dragging her into this mess and destroying what should have been a blissful time. Had they not chosen her, they would be sleeping soundly, her body next to his. Damn the Fates for cursing her and stealing her from him.

That foreign sensation slithered within him, and he clenched his hand tight at the anger it was bringing. Rolling his neck, he threw the bedsheets aside, intent on taking his wife as he should be and ignoring the world around him. Something in the air changed, and before he could rise, her body lurched forward.

All thoughts of anger fled, and he lunged from the bed, but she disappeared before he could reach her. She was gone. She hadn't shifted; he knew that caused no movement of the body. Shifting simply happened. This had been different as if she'd been taken, drawn from the room.

Fear crashed through him, filling all the spots where that foreign feeling had taken hold earlier. He ran like a madman through the castle, not caring that he remained shirtless and shoeless. He looked everywhere, trying to find her, to find Ren. Frustrated that he had found no one, Carnick made his way to the meeting room, where the fire was low, having burned down in the night. It was empty, no sign anyone had been there. He stood, his heart hammering in his chest, his mind running a thousand scenarios through it.

Finally, he calmed himself, knowing whatever had happened to her was beyond his power and likely his understanding. He prayed that she was safe, that the blasted Fates hadn't thrown her into a nightmare situation that brought harm to her. He listened as the storm howled against the windows, rattling them with the ferocity of a caged animal. There was a new intensity to it, and he was drawn to the windows, his eyes seeing the strange lights in the distance. Flickers of gold like the stars themselves were dropping from the sky. He rubbed his eyes, thinking he was seeing things, but when he reopened them, the same vision appeared. Stars didn't fall from the sky…unless. What had the immortals said, some of them returned to shine as stars high in the sky. Had those immortals been awoken? Had the battle begun? He hurried out of the meeting room, running to the castle doors and using his power to throw them open.

Briefly, he paused to stare at his hands. The doors were a wooden consistency, and wood was not something his family had control over. How had he moved them? It hadn't been a connection to the wood but more a force expelled from him. He turned back to them and willed them to shut, watching as they responded with a resounding thud that echoed through the strangely quiet night. That couldn't be. Only the immortals had that kind of magic. His eyes remained fixed on the doors, his mind trying to sort out this new ability when a flicker in the darkness drew his attention. He looked to the sky. It was pitch black with only the light of the moons which seemed distorted. He looked closer; the light was not distorted, but marred. Something massive had hit the moons, leaving damage across their surface. What could have caused such a thing to happen? His mind drifted to Xali's shared dream; she'd said there had only been one moon left, its appearance as if it had been wrenched violently in half.

The gods. They were here. Was that why Xali had disappeared? Was that why the stars had fallen? Had the war truly begun and Xali in the middle of it, vulnerable and defenseless? His heart hammered, thudding so loudly he thought it could be heard echoing through the silent space. Lights flickered where the mountains should have sat too far in the distance for him to see. But the lights were there, bouncing in and out of the dark. The sky was now starless, what had happened to them? Flashes of silver, gold, and red cast out across the horizon, and that strange feeling he'd been having stirred deep below again. For a moment, he almost lost his balance, the call to it was so strong. His powers crested within him in response, raised in defense to whatever the foreign feeling was, making it known that it was unwelcome. An internal battle ensued, a war that left him frozen with anticipation and fear. Whatever was happening within him seemed to be exacerbated by the battle in the distance, a call to something.

He clenched his hands, his breathing short, that feeling

spreading through him. All thoughts of Xali were lost, replaced with anger, ire, the need to harm, the need for vengeance. It roared through him, trying to latch onto the Dark side of his power. Just as he thought it would dominate him, he saw Ren and Xali coming through the darkness. They looked exhausted and defeated. That feeling in him stirred but settled, the relief at seeing Xali sending it back to where it had simmered. He didn't have time to question it as he ran to her, folding her shaking body into his arms.

He looked to Ren, the expression he wore one of a mix of emotions, his eyes a bright violet against the dark of the night.

"It has begun," Ren said. "The end is here."

Seventeen

The beautiful long room with the warming fireplace where once the immortals met to lead their kingdom had been transformed to a place of battle strategy. The flames that blazed no longer warming but instead throwing ominous shadows on the walls and over those within.

Relief flooded Carnick's face upon seeing Xali. She watched as he came to her and spoke of how he had awoken suddenly to see her as she was being ripped away. As he spoke, there was something below his words that told Xali something more had happened. She could sense the profound worry he had, but he was hiding something more like he'd had his own experience while she'd been summoned to witness the rise of the gods, the ensuing battle. What was happening to him? Fates, what was happening to all of them? She'd been in the grasp of a god, and he'd intended to murder her just as he had her aunt. The vision of her aunt's demise fluttered in her mind, causing her stomach to lurch once more. He hadn't killed Xali, however, and something about that gnawed at her mind as if she were missing an important piece of a puzzle that couldn't be finished without it. *Chaos*, it had called her, and the word had stuck. She was chaos, all of this brought on by her curiosity, her foolishness, her birth.

"Xali," Ren's voice woke her from her thoughts.

"I'm sorry, I didn't hear."

His brow raised, but it was empathy she saw in his face, not anger.

"Are you comfortable leading the protection of southern Cirillia, you and Carnick?"

"Cirillia? Why wouldn't we protect our own people?" Carnick asked.

"Your family will help with that," Ren said.

"But not me?" Xali asked.

"It's safer for you to be further from the mountains," Carnick said.

"Safer?"

"Yes," Ren answered. "You are a target, your aunts want you dead, and that god almost killed you."

"Aunt," she corrected. "There is only one left. And the god didn't kill me…he didn't."

"But he would have, Xali," Carnick argued. "And it's safer to have you as far away from their attention as we can. I agree with Ren."

"I'm not hiding on the edge of Old Cirillia"—Ren shot her a look—"Cirillia like a scared child."

Ren slammed his hand on the table, the force sending a crack through it. "But you are a child, a mortal child who can barely wield her powers, let alone protect herself."

The room was silent as she glared at his ebony eyes. "I am not a child, and I am not hiding in Cirillia, I will fight beside my people."

"Then you will die, and it will have all been for naught."

"What if you're with her?" Carnick asked.

Ren shook his head. "No, the bulk of the beasts are scattered throughout Tenebron and the northern ridges of Cirillia. I am needed here."

"I don't need protection," Xali said, exasperated. "They don't want me dead like my aunts did."

"That creature had you in its grasp."

"Yet it didn't kill me. They want me alive for some reason. You heard it, it asked me why it would kill me, and it killed her instead."

"They want you alive?" Cody asked, his eyes a brilliant blue.

"I don't think that's how it works," Ren said. "There was a reason it didn't kill you, but I guarantee the end goal is your death. It said it wasn't your time, that it wasn't the one to kill you. You're important to them, we just don't know why."

"I'll stay with her. I'll keep her healed if anything should happen," Cody offered.

"And can you fight those gods if they come after her?" Carnick asked.

"No, but she doesn't think they will."

"I'm not risking her life on what she thinks," Ren said.

"You're here because of what I think," Xali argued. "It was me who found you, who fought against what everyone was telling me. Call it—"

"Instinct," Ren finished with a grumble, before running his hands through his hair.

"Fine, Cody, you go with her. I want a Darkbearer with her though." He paused, and she could tell he was deliberating. "Damn, you'll cost me my two most experienced Council. Eoin, go with them. If anything happens you take her and Carnick and shift. You are not to fight anything but their minions. You will not win."

One by one, the room emptied. Her family would be spread throughout the realm to fight alongside Ren's men with what remaining power they had. As his Council left to collect them, she wondered how they would fare. Were they all destined to die in the end? Perhaps the Fates' plan had been that all along, culminating with her own death.

"If I had my way, you'd be locked in here safe with Paige," Ren said, bringing her thoughts back.

"Not a good idea to keep Xali from a fight," Carnick said.

"So, I'm learning."

"I'm right here," Xali said, irritated, "in case either of you forgot."

"I don't think that's something any of us can forget," Carnick said, giving her a sheepish grin.

"This isn't child's play, Xali," Ren said. "You saw what they can do, what they are."

"I felt it, remember, that one had me in its grasp."

"Then you would be wise to stay out of the fray."

"I don't think I have that choice, Ren."

"Aye, I think you're right," he said with a deep sigh. "Be safe and if any of them escape that mountain, you run. Understand?"

"Yes," she answered, but something gnawed at the edge of her consciousness, something that told her running was not her place, that she was meant to play a bigger part.

Ren shook his head sadly, his eyes now that startling blue. He shifted without a word, leaving her to wonder at his reaction.

"Guess it's time to fight," Carnick said.

"That it is," the one called Eoin said as he took Xali's arm, Cody doing the same to Carnick.

"Let's go see what mess lies in wait for us."

The world shifted, and they landed in the front hall of Xali's palace, or what had once been the front hall. Half of the walls were now rubble, fires burned across the open space, the stone gates nothing more than pebbles. Smoke plumed through the sky, billowing around them in a haze. She was thankful they'd thought to move her family to Ren's southern castle, otherwise, she suspected they'd be finding more than just the damaged palace.

"Good Fates," Eoin muttered.

Carnick grabbed Xali's arms, fear in his eyes.

"Ren was right, we need to be anywhere but here."

A shriek echoed through the air, sending chills across her spine.

"We should be very far from here, Xali," Carnick said.

"Carnick," she said, taking his hand, "this is my fight, too. You cannot keep me from it."

She ran her fingers through his silver hair, noticing that it hung longer than it had, disheveled from the moons of worry, of trying to keep her safe, always searching for her. He'd been on edge, they both had since the day she'd discovered the truth, perhaps even before that, their time made up of running, fighting for a peace, a quiet that didn't seem tangible. Would they ever have it? Would their lives ever be simple again? Had it ever been?

She reached up and kissed him, knowing there was no going back. This was her destiny, no matter the cost. No matter how it seemed to put a rift between them that grew wider each day, would it one day be too wide to cross?

"I love you," she whispered, "but this is my path. I was once told that you cannot run from it, for if you do, the price is costly."

"This price is too costly, Xali. You could die out there."

"I could die in another realm, Carnick. The Fates have tied me to this, and if I turn my back on that, if I run from it, what does that mean for us? For our world? What if I am the key that keeps this world together and I run from it?"

He dropped his head to touch hers, and she felt his resignation.

"I don't want to lose you. Seeing you so close to death, Xali, it was devastating. Something is waiting for you, and I don't want it to take you from me again."

A roar bellowed, shaking what was left of the front hall.

"I don't think we have a choice," she said, slowly pulling from his arms, her fingers the last to drop one by one from his hand.

He nodded, a shadow crossing his eyes, eclipsing the storm clouds, a slight flicker of red that gave her pause. The same shadow crossed his features. She didn't have time to evaluate it as Eoin interrupted.

"If you two are done, maybe we can fight that." He pointed to a beast that was loping from the distance, its black hide covered in what looked like tar, bits of lava gnawing throughout its tar fur. It stood six feet high and seemed the length of three stallions.

It stopped and turned, something drawing its attention. A horse and rider approached, and it roared again, the sound bringing pain to Xali's ears. The rider dismounted and the ground rose under the beast, toppling it. Xali squinted, recognizing Mendol's messy hair, the aura of his magic.

"It's Mendol!" she cried.

"What the Fates is he doing here?" Cody complained. "I thought your family was all in the southern castle?"

She had as well, but watching Mendol fight the beast, she recognized his determination and knew he had decided against their advice. She wondered if any of the others had done the same.

"We'd better help him," Eoin said, and he and Cody shifted to help, leaving them behind.

She moved to run toward the fight as a second beast flew down, throwing Eoin far across the grounds. Carnick grabbed her wrist tightly, and Xali turned to him, looking down at her wrist and then to him, her heart pounding as the red flecks slowly overtook the violet. "I thought we were helping, too," she said, shakily.

"Perhaps they feel the same as I," Carnick snapped.

She stepped back at his tone, a distinct shift from the one he'd had only moments before. His eyes were thunderous, the storm clouds in them black with shades of red against the gray they always held. The specks of violet now completely submerged below the storm. The same they had looked the night he'd tried to hurt her, lost to whatever pull he'd said he'd felt, the one she had not.

It was then she sensed it, a shroud of darkness around them, the same she'd noticed as the gods had emerged. It settled in the smoke that lay heavy on the air. She took a step back instinctively as the ground shook, and he released her wrist.

"Carnick," she whispered as the space around them grew black.

He didn't move, his eyes boring into hers. Eyes she'd gazed into since she was just a babe, ones that now sent a wave of terror through her.

"You wouldn't listen, Xaliandri." His voice was terse, deeper than normal, frightening. "I tried to warn you, tried to leave, to run with you, but you wouldn't listen."

He took a step forward, his aura transforming to a mist of black and red like the hide of the beast. Something grabbed her, snaking around her neck. "Now it's too late."

Her feet drifted from the floor, her throat constricting further as the force lifted her.

"You were wrong. You were all wrong. The Fates are using you. The gods are using you. But it was never just about you and your destiny. It was about mine, too. It's always been both of us, but you and your immortals were too wrapped up in yourselves to see it. Now, the true chaos begins."

He snapped his finger, and she heard the roar that answered, the beast leaping from nowhere, ripping her from the magic's hold and pinning her beneath its enormous paw.

She didn't struggle, the shock of Carnick's change heavy upon her. She noted the others fighting the other beasts in the distance, too many now for them to reach her. She heard the yelling as they realized she'd been hurt, felt the healing magic as Cody tried to heal her, felt the shredding of her soul with her skin as the beast's claws tore through her small body, but she never moved her eyes from Carnick's. No one noticed but she that he'd mounted the beast before it ripped its claws one final time across her chest.

Chaos has come, his voice slipped into her mind before the beast roared, wings spanning to send the others tumbling. She watched as it ascended, taking Carnick with it, stealing what was left of him, as her heart broke, the shattered pieces stilling her fight and her breathing until she could fight no more, and darkness claimed her.

J. L. Jackola discovered her passion for writing in grade school when she wrote a short story that earned her a spot in a local writing workshop. She has been creating fantasy worlds ever since. When she's not weaving tales, she can be found logging miles in her running shoes, watching movies with her family, or curled up with a book. She resides in Delaware with her husband and three children.

To learn more, visit her website at www.jljackola.com.